The Accident

The Accident

by ELIE WIESEL

translated from the French
by ANNE BORCHARDT

 HILL AND WANG
The Noonday Press
New York

For Paul Braunstein

Preface

In "The Myth of Sisyphus," Albert Camus declares that "there is only one truly serious philosophical problem: suicide." For the adolescent Jews of my wartime generation, it wasn't a question of philosophy. Our problem wasn't death but the dead. Wouldn't we be betraying them by choosing to integrate ourselves into the lives of others?

Michael Elkins, in *Forged in Fury*, tells how after the war hundreds of Jewish children in Poland allowed themselves to slip quietly into death. They had known how to fight hunger, conquer fear, and outmaneuver the myriad perils that had plagued them *during* the reign of Night. But once the world had more or less returned to "normal," they gave up. Out of despair? Perhaps out of weariness. They were abruptly forced to realize to what extent they were depleted. And vanquished. And stigmatized. And alone.

That is the theme of this novel. Entitled *Le jour (Day)*

in its original French version, it follows *Dawn* and *Night*. It is an ironic title, to be sure, indicating not the end of the darkness but its hold over those seeking to find a bit of warmth, a bit of light.

Although written in the first person, *The Accident* springs from my imagination. I speak for my protagonist, but he does not speak for me. He has lived through some of my experiences, but I have not lived through his. Nevertheless, we share an obsession with memory: memory is our home.

The wave of suicides that is breaking over today's youth gives this book a singular topicality and urgency. Must we be reminded that, in the end, all works of literature, even despairing ones, constitute an appeal to life?

ELIE WIESEL
New York, 1985

The Accident

"*I was once more struck by the truth of the ancient saying: Man's heart is a ditch full of blood. The loved ones who have died throw themselves down on the bank of this ditch to drink the blood and so come to life again; the dearer they are to you, the more of your blood they drink.*"

—NIKOS KAZANTZAKIS, *Zorba the Greek*

The accident occurred on an evening in July, right in the heart of New York, as Kathleen and I were crossing the street to go to see the movie *The Brothers Karamazov.*

The heat was heavy, suffocating: it penetrated your bones, your veins, your lungs. It was difficult to speak, even to breathe. Everything was covered with an enormous, wet sheet of air. The heat stuck to your skin, like a curse.

People walked clumsily, looking haggard, their mouths dry like the mouths of old men watching the decay of their existence; old men hoping to take leave of their own beings so as not to go mad. Their bodies filled them with disgust.

I was tired. I had just finished my work: a five-hundred word cable. Five hundred words to say nothing. To cover up another empty day. It was one of those quiet and monotonous Sundays that leave no mark on time. Washington: nothing. United Nations: nothing. New York:

nothing. Even Hollywood said: nothing. The movie stars had deserted the news.

It wasn't easy to use five hundred words to say that there was nothing to say. After two hours of hard work, I was exhausted.

"What shall we do now?" Kathleen asked.

"Whatever you like," I answered.

We were on the corner of Forty-fifth Street, right in front of the Sheraton-Astor. I felt stunned, heavy, a thick fog in my head. The slightest gesture was like trying to lift a planet. There was lead in my arms, in my legs.

To my right I could see the human whirlwind on Times Square. People go there as they go to the sea: neither to fight boredom nor the anguish of a room filled with blighted dreams, but to feel less alone, or more alone.

The world turned in slow motion under the weight of the heat. The picture seemed unreal. Beneath the colorful neon carnival, people went back and forth, laughing, singing, shouting, insulting one another, all of this with an exasperating slowness.

Three sailors had come out of the hotel. When they saw Kathleen they stopped short, and, in unison, gave a long admiring whistle.

"Let's go," Kathleen said, pulling me by the arm. She was obviously annoyed.

"What do you have against them?" I asked. "They think you're beautiful."

"I don't like them to whistle like that."

I said, in a professorial tone, "It's their way of looking at a woman: they see her with their mouths and not with their eyes. Sailors keep their eyes for the sea: when they are on land, they leave their eyes behind as tokens of love."

The three admirers had already been gone for quite some time.

"And you?" Kathleen asked. "How do you look at me?" She liked to relate everything to us. We were always the center of her universe. For her, other mortals lived only to be used as comparisons.

"I? I don't look at you," I answered, slightly annoyed. There was a silence. I was biting my tongue. "But I love you. You know that."

"You love me, but you don't look at me?" she asked gloomily. "Thanks for the compliment."

"You don't understand," I went right on. "One doesn't necessarily exclude the other. You can love God, but you can't look at Him."

She seemed satisfied with this comparison. I would have to practice lying.

"Whom do you look at when you love God?" she asked after a moment of silence.

"Yourself. If man could contemplate the face of God, he would stop loving him. God needs love; he does not need understanding."

"And you?"

For Kathleen, even God was not so much a subject for discussion as a way to bring the conversation back to us.

"I too," I lied. "I too, I need your love."

We were still in the same spot. Why hadn't we moved? I don't know. Perhaps we were waiting for the accident.

I'll have to learn to lie, I kept thinking. Even for the short time I have left. To lie well. Without blushing. Until then I had been lying much too badly. I was awkward, my face would betray me and I would start blushing.

"What are we waiting for?" Kathleen was getting impatient.

"Nothing," I said.

I was lying without knowing it: we were waiting for the accident.

"You still aren't hungry?"

"No," I answered.

"But you haven't eaten anything all day," she said reproachfully.

"No."

Kathleen sighed.

"How long do you think you can hold out? You're slowly killing yourself. . . ."

There was a small restaurant nearby. We went in. All right, I told myself. I'll also have to learn to eat. And to love. You can learn anything.

Ten or twelve people, sitting on high red stools, were eating silently at the counter. Kathleen now found herself in the crossfire of their stares. She was beautiful. Her face, especially around the lips, showed the first signs of a fear that was waiting for a chance to turn into live suffering. I would have liked to tell her once more that I loved her.

We ordered two hamburgers and two glasses of grapefruit juice.

"Eat," Kathleen said, and she looked up at me pleadingly.

I cut off a piece and lifted it to my mouth. The smell of blood turned my stomach. I felt like throwing up. Once I had seen a man eating with great appetite a slice of meat without bread. Starving, I watched him for a long time. As if hypnotized, I followed the motion of his fingers and jaws. I was hoping that if he saw me there, in front of him, he would throw me a piece. He didn't look up. The next day he was hanged by those who shared his barracks: he had been eating human flesh. To defend himself he had

screamed, "I didn't do any harm: he was already dead. . . ."
When I saw his body swinging in the latrine, I wondered,
"What if he had seen me?"

"Eat," Kathleen said.

I swallowed some juice.

"I'm not hungry," I said with an effort.

A few hours later the doctors told Kathleen, "He's
lucky. He'll suffer less because his stomach is empty. He
won't vomit so much."

"Let's go," I told Kathleen as I turned to leave.

I could feel it: another minute there and I'd faint.

I paid for the hamburgers and we left. Times Square
hadn't changed. False lights, artificial shadows. The same
anonymous crowd twisting and untwisting. In the bars and
in the stores, the same rock-'n'-roll tunes hitting away at
your temples with thousands of invisible little hammers.
The neon signs still announced that to drink this or that
was good for your health, for happiness, for the peace of
the world, of the soul, and of I don't know what else.

"Where would you like to go?" Kathleen inquired.

She pretended not to have noticed how pale I was. Who
knows, I thought. She too perhaps will learn how to lie.

"Far," I answered. "Very far."

"I'll go with you," she declared.

The sadness and bitterness of her voice filled me with
pity. Kathleen has changed, I told myself. She, who believed in defiance, in fighting, in hatred, had now chosen
to submit. She, who refused to follow any call that didn't
come from herself, now recognized defeat. I knew that our
suffering changes us. But I didn't know that it could also
destroy others.

"Of course," I said. "I won't go without you."

I was thinking: to go far away, where the roads leading

13

to simplicity are known not merely to a select group, but to all; where love, laughter, songs, and prayers carry with them neither anger nor shame; where I can think about myself without anguish, without contempt; where the wine, Kathleen, is pure and not mixed with the spit of corpses; where the dead live in cemeteries and not in the hearts and memories of men.

"Well?" Kathleen asked, pursuing her idea. "Where shall we go? We can't stand here all night."

"Let's go to the movies," I said.

It was still the best place. We wouldn't be alone. We would think about something else. We would be somewhere else.

Kathleen agreed. She would have preferred to go back to my place or to hers, but she understood my objection: it would be too hot, while the movie would be air-conditioned. I came to the conclusion that it wasn't so hard to lie.

"What shall we see?"

Kathleen looked around her, at the theatres that surround Times Square. Then she exclaimed excitedly, "*The Brothers Karamazov!* Let's see *The Brothers Karamazov.*"

It was playing on the other side of the square. We would have to cross two avenues. An ocean of cars and noises separated us from the movie.

"I'd rather see some other picture," I said. "I like Dostoevski too much."

Kathleen insisted: it was a good, great, extraordinary movie. Yul Brynner as Dmitri. It was a picture one had to see.

"I'd rather see an ordinary mystery," I said. "Something without philosophy, without metaphysics. It's too hot for intellectual exercises. Look, *Murder in Rio* is playing on

14

this side. Let's go to that. I'd love to know how they commit murders in Brazil."

Kathleen was stubborn. Once again, she wanted to test our love. If Dostoevski won, I loved her; otherwise I didn't. I glanced at her. Still the fear around her lips, the fear that was going to become suffering. Kathleen was beautiful when she suffered; her eyes were deeper, her voice warmer, fuller; her dark beauty was simpler and more human. Her suffering had a quality of saintliness. It was her way of offering herself. I couldn't see Kathleen suffer without telling her I loved her, as if love was the negation of evil. I had to stop her suffering.

"You really care that much?" I asked her. "You're really that anxious to see the good brothers Karamazov mistreated?"

Apparently she was. It was Yul Brynner or our love.

"In that case, let's go."

A triumphant smile, that lasted only a second, lit up her face. Her fingers gripped my arm as if to say: now I believe in what is happening to us.

We took three or four steps, to the edge of the sidewalk. We had to wait a little. Wait for the red light to become green, for the flow of cars to stop, for the policeman who was directing traffic to raise his hand, for the cab driver, unaware of the role he was going to play in a moment, to reach the appointed spot. We had to wait for the director's cue.

I turned around. The clock in the TWA window said 10:25.

"Come on," Kathleen decided, pulling me by the arm. "It's green."

We started to cross the street. Kathleen was walking faster than I. She was on my right, a few inches ahead of me at most. The Brothers Karamazov weren't very far away any more, but I didn't see them that night.

What did I hear first? The grotesque screeching of brakes or the shrill scream of a woman? I no longer remember.

When I came to, for a fraction of a second, I was lying on my back in the middle of the street. In a tarnished mirror a multitude of heads were bending over me. There were heads everywhere. Right, left, above, and even underneath. All of them alike. The same wide-open eyes reflecting fright and curiosity. The same lips whispering the same incomprehensible words.

An elderly man seemed to be saying something to me. I think it was not to move. He had close-cropped hair and a mustache. Kathleen no longer had the beautiful black hair that she was so proud of. Disfigured, her face had lost its youth. Her eyes, as if in the presence of death, had grown larger, and, incredibly enough, she had grown a mustache.

A dream, I told myself. Just a dream that I'll forget when I wake up. Otherwise, why should I be here, on the pavement? Why would these people be around me as if I were going to die? And why would Kathleen suddenly have a mustache?

Noises, coming from all directions, bounced against a curtain of fog they weren't able to penetrate. I couldn't make out anything that was being said. I would have liked to tell them not to talk, because I couldn't hear them. I was dreaming, while they were not. But I was unable to utter the slightest sound. The dream had made me deaf and mute.

A poem by Dylan Thomas—always the same one—kept coming back to me, about not going gently into the night, but to "rage, rage, against the dying of the light."

16

Scream? Deaf-mutes don't scream. They go gently into the night, lightly, timidly. They don't scream against the dying of the light. They can't: their mouths are full of blood.

It's useless to scream when your mouth is filled with blood: people see the blood but cannot hear you scream. That's why I was silent. And also because I was dreaming of a summer night when my body was frozen. The heat was sickening, the faces bent over me streaming with sweat—sweat falling in rhythmical drops—and yet I was dreaming that I was so cold I was dying. How can one cry out against a dream? How can one scream against the dying of the light, against life that grows cold, against blood flowing out?

It was only later, much later, when I was already out of danger, that Kathleen told me about the circumstances surrounding the accident.

A speeding cab approaching from the left had caught me, dragging me several yards. Kathleen had suddenly heard the screeching of brakes and a woman's shrill scream.

She barely had time to turn around before a crowd was already surrounding me. She didn't know at first that I was the man lying at the spectators' feet.

Then, having a strong feeling that it was I, she pushed her way through and saw me: crushed with pain, curled up, my head between my knees.

And the people were talking, talking endlessly. . . .

"He's dead," one of them said.

"No, he's not. Look, he's moving."

Preceded by the sound of sirens, the ambulance arrived within twenty minutes. During that time I showed few signs of life. I didn't cry, I didn't moan, I didn't say anything.

In the ambulance I came to several times for a few seconds. During these brief moments I gave Kathleen astonishingly precise instructions about things I wanted her to do for me: inform the paper; call one of my friends and ask him to replace me temporarily; cancel various appointments; pay the rent, the phone bill, the laundry. Having handed her the last of these immediate problems, I closed my eyes and didn't open them again for five days.

Kathleen also told me this: the first hospital to which the ambulance took me refused to let me in. There wasn't any room. All the beds were taken. At least that's what they said. But Kathleen thought it was just a pretext. The doctors, after one glance at me, had decided there was no hope. It was better to be rid of a dying man as fast as possible.

The ambulance drove on to New York Hospital. Here, it seemed, they weren't afraid of the dying. The doctor on duty, a composed and sympathetic-looking young resident, immediately took care of me while trying to make a diagnosis.

"Well, Doctor?" Kathleen had asked.

Through some miracle she hadn't been sent out of the emergency room while Dr. Paul Russel was taking care of me.

"At first sight it looks rather bad," the young doctor answered.

And he explained in a professional tone, "All the bones on the left side of his body are broken; internal hemorrhage; brain concussion; I can't tell about his eyes yet; whether they'll be affected or not. The same for his brain: let's hope it hasn't been damaged."

Kathleen tried not to cry.

"What can be done, Doctor?"

"Pray."

"Is it that serious?"

"Very serious."

The young doctor, whose voice was as restrained as an old man's, looked at her for a moment, then asked, "Who are you? His wife?"

On the verge of hysteria, Kathleen just shook her head to say no.

"His fiancée?"

"No," she whispered.

"His girl friend?"

"Yes."

After hesitating a moment, he had asked her softly, "Do you love him?"

"Yes," Kathleen whispered.

"In that case, there are good reasons not to lose hope. Love is worth as much as prayer. Sometimes more."

Then Kathleen burst into tears.

After three days of consulting and waiting, the doctors decided that it was worth trying surgery after all. In any case I didn't have much to lose. On the other hand, with luck, if all went well . . .

The operation lasted a long time. More than five hours. Two surgeons had to take turns. My pulse fell dangerously low, I was almost given up for dead. With blood transfusions, shots, and oxygen, they brought me back to life.

Finally the surgeons decided to limit the operation to the hip. The ankle, the ribs, and the other small fractures could wait. The vital thing for the time being was to stop the bleeding, sew together the torn arteries, and close the incision.

I was brought back to my room and for two days swung between life and death. Dr. Russel, who was devotedly taking care of me, was still pessimistic about the final result. My fever was too high and I was losing too much blood.

On the fifth day I at last regained consciousness.

I'll always remember: I opened my eyes and had to close them right away because I was blinded by the whiteness of the room. A few minutes went by before I could open them again and locate myself in time and space.

On both sides of my bed there were bottles of plasma hanging from the wall. I couldn't move my arms: two big needles were fastened to them with surgical tape. Everything was ready for an emergency transfusion.

I tried to move my legs: my body no longer obeyed me. I felt a sudden fear of being paralyzed. I made a superhuman effort to shout, to call a nurse, a doctor, a human being, to ask for the truth. But I was too weak. The sounds stuck in my throat. Maybe I've lost my voice too, I thought.

I felt alone, abandoned. Deep inside I discovered a regret: I would have preferred to die.

An hour later, Dr. Russel came into the room and told me I was going to live. My legs were not going to be amputated. I couldn't move them because they were in a cast that covered my whole body. Only my head, my arms, my toes, were visible.

"You've come back from very far," the young doctor said.

I didn't answer. I still felt regret at having come back from so far.

"You must thank God," he went on.

I looked at him more carefully. Sitting on the edge of my bed, his fingers intertwined, his eyes were filled with an intense curiosity.

"How does one thank God?" I asked him.

My voice was only a whisper. But I was able to speak. This filled me with such joy that tears came to my eyes. That I was still alive had left me indifferent, or nearly so. But the knowledge that I could still speak filled me with an emotion that I couldn't hide.

The doctor had a wrinkled baby face. He was blond. His light blue eyes showed a great deal of goodness. He was looking at me very attentively. But this didn't bother me. I was too weak.

"How does one thank God?" I repeated.

I would have liked to add: why thank him? I had not been able to understand for a long time what in the world God had done to deserve man.

The doctor continued to look at me closely, very closely. A strange gleam—perhaps a strange shadow—was in his eyes.

Suddenly my heart jumped. Frightened, I thought: he knows something.

"Are you cold?" he asked, still looking at me.

"Yes," I answered, worried. "I'm cold."

My body was trembling.

"It's your fever," he explained.

Usually they take your pulse. Or else they touch your forehead with the back of their hand. He did nothing. He knew.

"We'll try to fight the fever," he went on sententiously. "We'll give you shots. Many shots. Penicillin. Every hour. Day and night. The enemy now is fever."

He stopped talking and looked at me for a long time before going on. He seemed to be looking for a sign, an indication, a solution to a problem whose particulars I couldn't guess.

"We're afraid of infection," he continued. "If the fever goes up, you're lost."

"And the enemy will be victorious," I said in a tone of voice that intended irony. "You see, Doctor, what people say is true: man carries his fiercest enemy within himself. Hell isn't others. It's ourselves. Hell is the burning fever that makes you feel cold."

An indefinable bond had grown between us. We were speaking the mature language of men who are in direct contact with death. I tried to put on a smile but, being too cold, I could only manage a grin. That's one reason why I don't like winter: smiles become abstract.

Dr. Russel got up.

"I'll send the nurse. It's time for a shot."

He was touching his lips with his fingers, as if to think better, and then added, "When you feel better, we'll have a lot to talk about."

Again I had the uncomfortable impression that he knew —or at least that he suspected—something.

I closed my eyes. Suddenly I became conscious of the pain that was torturing me. I had not realized it before. And yet the suffering was there. It was the air I was breathing, the words forming in my brain, the cast that covered my body like a flaming skin. How had I managed to remain unaware of it until then? Perhaps I had been too absorbed in the conversation with the doctor. Did he know I was suffering, suffering horribly? Did he know I was cold? Did he know that the suffering was burning my flesh and

22

that at the same time I was shaking with an unbearable cold, as if I were being plunged first into a furnace and then into an icy tub? Apparently he did. He knew. Paul Russel was a perceptive doctor. He could see me biting my lips furiously.

"You're in pain," he stated.

He was standing motionless at the foot of my bed. I was ashamed that my teeth were chattering in his presence.

"It's normal," he went on without waiting for an answer. "You're covered with wounds. Your body is rebelling. Pain is your body's way of protesting. But I told you: suffering is not the enemy, the fever is. If it goes up you are lost."

Death. I was thinking: He thinks that death is my enemy. He's mistaken. Death is not my enemy. If he doesn't know that, he knows nothing. Or at least he doesn't know everything. He has seen me come back to life, but he doesn't know what I think of life and death. Or could he possibly know and not show it? Doubt, like the insistent buzz of a bee inside me, was putting my nerves on edge.

I could feel the fever, as it spread, seize me by the hair, which seemed like a burning torch. The fever was throwing me from one world into another, up and down, very high up and very far down, as if it meant to teach me the cold of high places and the heat of abysses.

"Would you like a sedative?" the doctor inquired.

I shook my head. No, I didn't want any. I didn't need any. I wasn't afraid.

I heard his steps moving toward the door, which must have been somewhere behind me. Let him go, I thought. I'm not afraid of being alone, of walking the distance between life and death. No, I don't need him. I'm not afraid. Let him go!

He opened the door, hesitated before closing it. He stopped. Was he going to come back?

"Incidentally," he said softly, so softly I could hardly hear him. "Incidentally, I nearly forgot to tell you . . . Kathleen . . . she's an extremely charming young woman. Extremely charming . . ."

With that he quietly left the room. Now I was alone. Alone as only a paralyzed and suffering man can be. Soon the nurse would come, with her penicillin, to fight the enemy. It was maddening: to fight the enemy with an injection, with the help of a nurse. It was laughable. But I didn't laugh. The muscles in my face were motionless, frozen.

The nurse was going to come soon. That's what the young doctor had said, the doctor whose calm voice was like an old man's, having just discovered that human goodness carries its own reward. What else had he told me? Something about Kathleen. Yes: he had mentioned her name. Charming young woman. No. Not that. He had said something else: extremely charming. Yes: that's it. That's what he had said: Kathleen is a charming young woman. I remembered perfectly: extremely charming.

Kathleen . . . Where could she be now? In what world? In the one above or the one below? I hope she won't come. I hope she won't appear in this room. I don't want her to see me like this. I hope she won't come with the nurse. I hope she won't become a nurse. And that she won't give me penicillin. I don't want her help in my fight against the enemy. She's a charming girl, extremely charming, but she doesn't understand. She doesn't understand that death is not the enemy. That would be too easy. She doesn't understand. She has too much faith in the power, in the omnipotence of love. Love me and you'll be protected. Love each other and all will be well: suffering will leave man's earth forever. Who said that? Christ probably. He also believed too much in love. As for me, love or death. I didn't care. I was able to laugh when I thought about either. Now too, I could burst out laughing. Yes, but the muscles in my face didn't obey me. I was too cold.

It had been cold on the day—no, the evening—that evening when I met Kathleen for the first time.

A winter evening. Outside, a wind sharp enough to cut through walls and trees.

"Come along," Shimon Yanai told me. "I'd like you to meet Halina."

"Let me listen to the wind," I answered (I wasn't in a talkative mood). "The wind has more to say than your Halina. The sound of the wind carries the regrets and prayers of dead souls. Dead souls have more to say than living ones."

Shimon Yanai—the most beautiful mustache in Palestine, not to say in the whole Middle East—wasn't paying any attention to what I was saying.

"Come," he said, his hands in his pockets. "Halina is waiting for us."

I gave in. I thought: perhaps Halina is a dead soul too.

We were standing in the lobby during an intermission

at the ballet in Paris, the Roland Petit Company or the Marquis de Cuevas, I no longer remember.

"Halina must be an attractive woman," I said as we crossed the lobby to get to the bar.

"What makes you think that?" asked Shimon Yanai, who seemed amused.

"The way you're dressed tonight. You look like a bum." I liked to tease him. Shimon was in his forties, tall, bushy hair, blue and dreamy eyes. He never wanted to be taken seriously. "You spend hours in front of the mirror mussing your hair, spoiling the knot in your tie, rumpling your trousers," I would often tell him, ironically but with affection. There was something pathetic about his love for the Bohemian.

I knew him well because he came to Paris often and gave me tips for the newspaper. He liked to be with journalists. He needed them. He was the Paris representative of the Hebrew Resistance Movement—the state of Israel hadn't been born yet—and he didn't hesitate to admit that the press could be helpful to him.

Halina was waiting for us at the bar, a glass in her hand. She was thirtyish. Thin, narrow face, pale, with the eternally frightened look of a woman fighting with her past.

We shook hands.

"I thought you'd be older." She was smiling awkwardly.

"I am," I said. "At times I am as old as the wind."

Halina laughed. She didn't really know how to laugh. When she laughed, she could break your heart. Her laughter was as haunting as a dead soul.

"I'm serious," she said. "I read your articles. They are written by a man who has come to the end of his life, to the end of his hopes."

"That is a sign of youth," I answered. "The young today don't believe that some day they'll be old: they are convinced they'll die young. Old men are the real youngsters of our generation. They at least can brag about having had what we do not have: a slice of life called youth."

The young woman's face became still paler. "What you are saying is dreadful."

I burst out laughing, but my laughter must have sounded forced: I didn't feel like laughing. Not any more than like talking.

"Don't listen to me," I said. "Shimon will tell you: my words are never serious. I am playing, that's all. Playing at frightening you. But you mustn't pay any attention. What I'm saying is just wind."

I was going to leave them—on the usual pretext of an urgent phone call to make—when I noticed a worried look in Halina's eyes.

"Shimon!" she exclaimed without raising her voice. "Look who is here: Kathleen!"

Shimon looked where she was pointing and for a second —only a second—his face clouded over. His cheeks darkened, as if from a painful memory.

"Go and ask her to join us," Halina said.

"But she's not alone. . . ."

"Just for a minute! She'll come."

She did come. And that's when it all started.

Actually I could easily have left while Shimon was talking to her at the other end of the lobby. My phone call was just as urgent then as it had been before. I didn't at all feel like staying. At first glance it looked like the classic situation. Three characters: Shimon, Halina, Kathleen. Halina loves Shimon who doesn't love her; Shimon loves Kathleen who does not love him; Kathleen loves . . . I didn't know whom she loved and cared less. I was thinking: they make one another suffer, in a tightly closed circle. Better not to have anything to do with it, not even as a witness. I'd never been interested in sterile suffering. Other people's suffering only attracts me to the extent that it allows man to become conscious of his strength and of his weakness, in a climate that favors rebellion. The loves of Halina and Shimon allowed nothing of the kind.

"I have to go," I told Halina.

She looked at me but didn't hear; she was watching Shimon and Kathleen at the end of the lobby.

"I have to go," I said again.

She seemed to come out of a dream, surprised to see me next to her. "Please stay," she asked in a humble, almost humiliated tone of voice. Then she added, either to convince me or to stress her indifference. "You're going to meet Kathleen. She is an extraordinary girl. You'll see."

It had become useless to resist: Kathleen and Shimon were there.

"Hello, Halina," Kathleen said in French with a strong American accent.

"Hello, Kathleen," Halina answered, barely hiding a certain nervousness. "Let me introduce a friend. . . ."

Without a gesture, without a move, without saying a word, Kathleen and I looked at each other for a long time, as if to establish a direct contact. She had a long, symmetrical face, uncommonly beautiful and touching. Her nose turned up slightly, accentuating her sensuous lips. Her almond-shaped eyes were filled with a dark, secret fire: an inactive volcano. With her, there could be real communication. All of a sudden I understood why Halina's laughter wasn't more carefree.

"You already know each other?" Halina asked with her awkward smile. "You look at each other as if you knew each other."

Shimon was silent. He was looking at Kathleen.

"Yes," I answered.

"What?" Halina exclaimed, not quite believing it. "You've already met?"

"No," I answered. "But we already know each other."

An imperceptible quiver went through Shimon's mustache. The situation was becoming unpleasantly tense when a warning bell suddenly rang. The intermission was over. The lobby began to empty.

"Shall we see you after the show?" Halina asked.

"I'm afraid not," Kathleen answered. "Someone is waiting for me."

"And you?" Halina looked at me, her big eyes filled with a cold sadness.

"No," I answered. "I have to make a phone call. It's urgent."

Halina and Shimon went off. We were alone, Kathleen and I.

"Do you speak English?" she asked me in English, as if in a hurry.

"I do."

"Wait for me," she said.

She walked quickly to the man who was waiting at the other end of the lobby, said a few words to him. I still had a chance to leave. But why run away? And where to? The desert is the same everywhere. Souls die in it. And sometimes they play at killing the souls that are not yet dead.

When Kathleen came back a few seconds later, I saw a fleeting expression of defiance and decision on her face, as if she had just completed the most important act in her life. The man she had just left and humiliated remained completely motionless and stiff, as if struck by a curse.

Inside, the curtain had gone up.

"Let's leave," Kathleen said in English.

I felt like asking endless questions, but decided to keep them for later.

"All right," I said. "Let's leave."

We left the lobby hurriedly. The man stayed behind alone. For a long time after I was afraid to go back to that theatre. I was afraid of finding him there, on the very spot where we had left him.

We went down the stairs, got our coats, and went out into the street where the wind whipped us angrily. The air was clear and pure, as it is on the peaks of snowy mountains.

We began to walk. It was cold. We were advancing slowly, as if to prove that we were strong and that the cold had no power over us.

Kathleen hadn't taken my arm and I hadn't taken hers. She didn't look at me and I didn't look at her. Either of us would have gone on walking at the same pace if the other had stopped suddenly to think, or to pray.

After walking silently along the Seine for an hour or two, we crossed the Pont du Châtelet, and then, when we reached the middle of the Pont Saint-Michel, I stopped to look at the river. Kathleen took two more steps and stopped too.

The Seine, reflecting the sky and the lampposts, now showed us its mysterious winter face, its quiet cloudiness, where any life is extinguished, where any light dies. I looked down and thought that someday I too would die.

Kathleen came closer and was about to say something. With a motion of my head, I stopped her.

"Don't talk," I told her after a while.

I was still thinking about death and didn't want her to talk to me. It is only in silence, leaning over a river in winter, that one can really think about death.

One day I had asked my grandmother, "How should one keep from being cold in a grave in the winter?"

My grandmother was a simple, pious woman who saw God everywhere, even in evil, even in punishment, even in injustice. No event would ever find her short of prayers. Her skin was like white desert sand. On her head she wore an enormous black shawl which she never seemed able to part with.

"He who doesn't forget God isn't cold in his grave," she said.

"What keeps him warm?" I insisted.

Her thin voice had become like a whisper: it was a secret. "God himself." A kind smile lit up her face all the way to the shawl that covered half her forehead. She smiled like that every time I asked her a question with an obvious answer.

"Does that mean that God is in the grave, with the men and the women that are buried?"

"Yes," my grandmother assured me. "It is he who keeps them warm."

I remember that then a strange sadness came upon me. I felt pity for God. I thought: he is more unhappy than man, who dies only once, who is buried in only one grave.

"Grandma, tell me, does God die too?"

"No, God is immortal."

Her answer came as a blow. I felt like crying. God was buried alive! I would have preferred to reverse the roles, to think that God is mortal and man not. To think that, when man acts as if he were dying, it is God who is covered with earth.

Kathleen touched my arm. I jumped.

"Don't touch me," I told her. I was thinking of my grandmother and you cannot truly remember a dead grandmother if you aren't alone, if a girl with black hair—black like my grandmother's shawl—touches your arm.

Suddenly it occurred to me that my grandmother's smile had a meaning that the future was to reveal: she knew that my question did not concern her, that she would not know the cold of a grave. Her body had not been buried, but entrusted to the wind that had blown it in all directions. And it was her body—my grandmother's white and black body—that whipped my face, as if to punish me for having forgotten. No, Grandmother! No! I haven't forgotten. Every time I'm cold, I think of you, I think only of you.

"Come on," Kathleen said. "Let's go. I'm getting cold."

We started walking again. The wind cut our faces, but we went on. We didn't walk faster. Finally we stopped on Boulevard Saint-Germain, opposite the Deux-Magots.

"Here we are," she said.

"This is where you live?"

"Yes. Do you want to come up?"

I had to fight against myself not to say no. I wanted to stay with her too much, to talk to her, to touch her hair, to see her fall asleep. But I was afraid of being disappointed.

"Come," Kathleen insisted.

She opened the heavy door and we walked up one flight to her apartment.

I was cold. And I was thinking of my grandmother whose face was white like the transparent desert sand, and whose shawl was as black as the dense night of cemeteries.

Who are you?"

I could hardly hear my own voice. Thousands of needles were injecting fire into my blood. I was thirsty. I felt hot. My throat was dry. My veins were about to burst. And yet the cold hadn't left me. My body, shaken by convulsions, trembled like a tree in a storm, like leaves in the wind, like the wind in the sea, like the sea in the head of a madman, of a drunkard, of a dying man.

"Who are you?" I asked again, while my teeth chattered. I could feel there was someone in the room.

"The nurse," said an unknown voice.

"Water," I said. "I'm thirsty. I'm burning. Please give me some water."

"You mustn't drink," the voice said. "You'll feel bad. If you drink, you'll throw up."

Against my will, I began to cry silently.

"There, now," the nurse said. "I'm going to moisten your face."

34

She wiped my forehead and then my lips with a wet towel which caught fire as it touched my skin.

"What time is it?" I asked.

"Six o'clock."

"At night?"

"Yes."

I thought: when Dr. Russel came to see me, it was well before noon. Six penicillin shots, I hadn't even noticed.

"Are you in pain?" the nurse asked.

"I'm thirsty."

"It's the fever that's making you thirsty."

"Do I still have a high fever?"

"Yes."

"How high?"

"High."

"I want to know."

"I'm not allowed to tell you. That's the rule."

The door opened. Someone came in. Whispers.

"Well, my friend? What have you got to say?"

Dr. Russel was trying to be casual.

"I'm thirsty, Doctor."

"The enemy refuses to retreat," he said. "It's up to you to hold out."

"He'll win, Doctor. He doesn't suffer from thirst."

I thought: Grandmother would have understood. It was hot in the airless, waterless chambers. It was hot in the room where her livid body was crushed by other livid bodies. Like me, she must have opened her mouth to drink air, to drink water. But there was no water where she was, there was no air. She was only drinking death, as you drink water or air, mouth open, eyes closed, fingers clenched.

Suddenly I felt a strange need to speak out loud. To tell the story of Grandmother's life and death, to describe

her black shawl that used to frighten me until I was reassured by her kind, simple expression. Grandmother was
my refuge. Every time my father scolded me, she would
intervene: fathers are like that, she'd explain smilingly.
They get angry over nothing.

One day my father slapped me. I had stolen some money
from the store cash register in order to give it to a class-
mate. A sickly, poor little boy. They called him Haïm the
orphan. I always felt ill at ease in his presence. I knew I
was happier than he was and this made me feel guilty.
Guilty that my parents were alive. That's why I stole the
money. But when my father asked me, trying to find out
what I had done with it, I didn't tell him. After all, I
couldn't tell my father that I felt guilty because he was
alive! He slapped my face and I ran to Grandmother.
I could tell her the whole truth. She didn't scold me. Sitting in the middle of the room, she lifted me onto her lap
and began to sob. Her tears fell on my head, which she was
holding against her bosom, and I discovered to my surprise
that a grandmother's tears are so hot that they burn everything in their path.

"She's there," the doctor said. "She's outside. In the
hallway. Do you want her to come in?"

With the strength that came from my fear, I screamed,
"No! I don't, I don't."

I thought he was talking about my grandmother. I didn't
want to see her. I knew she had died—of thirst, maybe—
and I was afraid she wouldn't be as I remembered her. I
was afraid she wouldn't have the black shawl on her head,
nor those burning tears in her eyes, nor that clear, calm
expression that could make you forget you were cold.

"You should see her," the doctor said softly.

"No! Not now!"

My tears left scars on my cheeks, on my lips, on my chin. From time to time, they even managed to slip under the cast. Why was I crying? I had no idea. I think it was because of Grandmother. She used to cry very often. She would cry when she was happy and also when she was unhappy. When she was neither happy nor unhappy, she would cry because she could no longer feel the things that bring about happiness and unhappiness. I wanted to prove to her that I had inherited her tears, which, as it is written, open all doors.

"It's up to you," the doctor said. "Kathleen can come back tomorrow."

Kathleen! What did she have to do with this? How did she meet Grandmother? Had she also died?

"Kathleen?" I said, letting my head fall back. "Where is she?"

"Outside," the doctor said somewhat surprised. "In the hallway."

"Bring her in."

The door opened and light footsteps came toward my bed. Again I made a desperate effort to open my eyes, but my eyelids felt sewn together.

"How are you, Kathleen?" I asked in a barely audible voice.

"Fine."

"You see: I am Dmitri Karamazov's most recent victim."

Kathleen forced a little laugh.

"You were right. It's a bad movie."

"Better to die than to see it."

Kathleen's laugh sounded false.

"You're exaggerating. . . ."

Whispers. The doctor was speaking to her very softly.

"I have to leave you," Kathleen said, sounding very sorry.

"Be careful crossing the street."

She leaned over to kiss me. An old fear took hold of me.

"You mustn't kiss me, Kathleen!"

She pulled back her head abruptly. For a moment there was silence in the room. Then I felt her hand on my forehead. I was going to tell her to take it away quickly and not to run the risk of catching fire, but she had already taken it away.

Kathleen tiptoed out of the room, followed by the doctor. The nurse stayed with me. I would really have liked to know what she looked like: old or young, beautiful or sullen, blond or brunette. . . . But I still couldn't move my eyelids. All my efforts to open them came to nothing. At one point I told myself that will power wasn't enough, that I had to use both my hands. But they were tied to the sides of the bed and the big needles were still there.

"I'm going to give you two shots," the nurse announced in a voice from which I could guess nothing.

"Two? Why two?"

"First penicillin. And the second to help you fall asleep."

"You don't have a third one against thirst?" I had a hard time breathing. My lungs were going to burst: empty kettles forgotten on the fire.

"You'll sleep. You won't be thirsty."

"I won't dream that I'm thirsty?"

The nurse lifted the covers. "I'll give you a shot against dreams."

She's nice, I thought. Her heart is made of gold. She suffers when I suffer. She's quiet when I'm thirsty. She's quiet when I sleep. She's quiet when I dream. She is probably young, beautiful, beaming, attractive. She has a serious face, laughing eyes. She has a sensual mouth, made for kissing, not for talking. Just like Grandmother's eyes, which she used not for looking, not for wondering, but simply for crying.

First shot. Nothing. I didn't feel it. Second shot, this one in the arm. Still nothing. I had so much pain that I couldn't even feel the injection.

The nurse fixed the covers, put the needles in a metal box, moved a chair, and turned a switch.

"I'm putting out the light," she said. "You'll go to sleep soon."

All at once I got the idea that she too would want to kiss me before leaving. Just a little meaningless kiss on the forehead or on the cheek and maybe even on the eyelids. They do that in hospitals. A good nurse kisses her patients when she says good night. Not on the mouth. On the forehead, on the cheeks. It reassures them. A patient thinks he is less ill if a woman wants to kiss him. He doesn't know that a nurse's mouth isn't made for speaking, or even for crying, but for keeping quiet and for kissing patients so they can fall asleep without fear, without fear of the dark.

Again, I was completely covered with perspiration.

"You mustn't kiss me," I whispered.

The nurse laughed in a friendly way.

"Of course not. It makes you thirsty."

Then she left the room. And I waited to fall asleep.

Tell me a little about yourself," Kathleen said.

We were sitting in her room where it was pleasantly warm. We were listening to a Gregorian chant, which swelled inside us. The words and the music contained a peace that no storm could have disturbed.

On a small table, our two cups were still half full. The coffee had become cold. The semidarkness made me keep my eyes closed. The feeling of exhaustion that had been weighing me down at the beginning of the evening had completely disappeared. My nerves tense, I was conscious that time, as it passed through me, was carrying a part of me along with it.

"Tell me," Kathleen said. "I want to know you."

Her legs folded under her, she was sitting on my right on the beige couch. A dream was floating in the air, looking for a place on which to settle.

"I don't feel like it," I answered. "I don't feel like talking about myself."

To talk about myself, really talk about myself, I would have had to tell the story of my grandmother. I didn't feel like expressing it in words: Grandmother could only be expressed in prayers.

After the war, when I arrived in Paris, I had often, very often, been urged to tell. I refused. I told myself that the dead didn't need us to be heard. They are less bashful than I. Shame has no hold on them, while I was bashful and ashamed. That's the way it is: shame tortures not the executioners but their victims. The greatest shame is to have been chosen by destiny. Man prefers to blame himself for all possible sins and crimes rather than come to the conclusion that God is capable of the most flagrant injustice. I still blush every time I think of the way God makes fun of human beings, his favorite toys.

Once I asked my teacher, Kalman the cabalist, the following question: For what purpose did God create man? I understand that man needs God. But what need of man has God?

My teacher closed his eyes and a thousand wounds, petrified arteries traveled by terror-stricken truths, drew a tangled labyrinth on his forehead. After a few minutes of contemplation, his lips formed a delicate, very distant smile.

"The Holy Books teach us," he said, "that if man were conscious of his power, he would lose his faith or his reason. For man carries within him a role which transcends him. God needs him to be ONE. The Messiah, called to liberate man, can only be liberated by him. We know that not only man and the universe will be freed, but also the one who established their laws and their relations. It

41

follows that man—who is nothing but a handful of earth —is capable of reuniting time and its source, and of giving back to God his own image."

At the time I was too young to understand the meaning of my teacher's words. The idea that God's existence could be bound to mine had filled me with a miserable pride as well as a deep pity.

A few years later I saw just, pious men walking to their death, singing, "We are going to break, with our fire, the chains of the Messiah in exile." That's when the symbolic implication of what my teacher had said struck me. Yes, God needs man. Condemned to eternal solitude, he made man only to use him as a toy, to amuse himself. That's what philosophers and poets have refused to admit: in the beginning there was neither the Word, nor Love, but laughter, the roaring, eternal laughter whose echoes are more deceitful than the mirages of the desert.

"I want to know you," Kathleen said.

Her face had darkened. The dream, finding no place to settle, had dissolved. I thought: it could have entered her wide-open eyes. But dreams never enter from outside.

"You might end up hating me," I told her.

She drew her legs under her still more. Her whole body contracted, became smaller, as if it had wanted to follow the dream and disappear altogether.

"I'll take a chance," she answered.

She'll hate me, I thought. It is unavoidable. What happened will happen again. The same causes bring about the same effects, the same hatreds. Repetition is a decisive factor in the tragic aspect of our condition.

I don't know the name of the first man who openly cried out his hatred to me, nor who he was. He represented all the nameless and faceless people who live in the universe of dead souls.

I was on a French ship sailing to South America. It was my first encounter with the sea. Most of the time I was on deck, studying the waves which, untiringly, dug graves only to fill them again. As a child I had searched for God because I imagined him great and powerful, immense and infinite. The sea gave me such an image. Now I understood Narcissus: he hadn't fallen into the fountain. He had jumped into it. At one point my desire to be one with the sea became so strong that I nearly jumped overboard.

I had nothing to lose, nothing to regret. I wasn't bound to the world of men. All I had cared for had been dispersed by smoke. The little house with its cracked walls, where children and old men came humming to pray or study in the melancholy light of candles, was nothing but ruins. My teacher, who had been the first to teach me that life is a mystery, that beyond words there is silence, my teacher, whose head was always hanging as if he didn't dare face heaven—my teacher had long since been reduced to ashes. And my little sister, who made fun of me because I never played with her, because I was too serious, much too serious, my little sister no longer played.

It was a stranger who, unknowingly, unwittingly, had prevented me from giving up that night. As I stood at the rail he had come up behind me, I don't know from where, and had started talking to me. He was an Englishman.

"Beautiful night," he said, leaning against the railing on my right, nearly touching me.

"Very beautiful," I answered coldly.

I thought: beautiful night for saying good-bye to cheaters, to the constants that become uncertainties, to ideals which imply treason, to the world where there is no longer room for what is human, to history that leads to the destruction of the soul instead of broadening its powers!

The stranger wasn't intimidated by my ill-humor. He continued. "The sky is so close to the sea that it is difficult to tell which is reflected in the other, which one needs the other, which one is dominating the other."

"That's true," I again answered coldly.

He stopped for a moment. I could see his profile: thin, sharp, noble.

"If the two were at war," he went on, "I'd be on the side of the sea. The sky only inspires painters. Not musicians. While the sea . . . Don't you feel that the sea comes close to man through its music?"

"Perhaps," I answered with hostility.

Again he stopped, as if wondering if he shouldn't leave me alone. He decided to stay.

"Cigarette?" he asked, holding out his pack.

"No thanks. I don't feel like smoking."

He lit his cigarette and threw the match overboard: a shooting star swallowed up by darkness.

"They're dancing inside," he said. "Why don't you join them?"

"I don't feel like dancing."

"You prefer to be alone with the sea, don't you?"

His voice had suddenly changed. It had become more personal, less anonymous. I wasn't aware that a man could change his voice, as he would change a mask.

"Yes, I prefer to remain alone with the sea," I answered nastily, stressing the word "alone."

He took a few puffs on his cigarette.

"The sea. What does it make you think of?"

I hesitated. The fact that he was shrouded in darkness, that I didn't know him, that I probably wouldn't even recognize him the next day in the dining room, worked in his favor. To talk to a stranger is like talking to stars: it doesn't commit you.

"The sea," I said, "makes me think of death."

I had the impression that he smiled.

"I knew it."

"How did you know?" I asked, disconcerted.

"The sea has a power of attraction. I am fifty and have been traveling for thirty years. I know all the seas in the world. I know. One mustn't look at the waves for too long. Especially at night. Especially alone."

He told me about his first trip. His wife was with him. They had just gotten married. One night he left his wife, who was sleeping, and went up on deck to get some air. There he became aware of the terrible power of the sea over those who see in it their transformed silhouette. He was happy and young; and yet he felt a nearly irresistible need to jump, to be carried away by the living waves whose roar, more than anything else, evokes eternity, peace, the infinite.

"I'm telling you," he repeated very softly. "One mustn't look at the sea for too long. Not alone, and not at night."

Then I too started telling him things about myself. Knowing that he had thought about death and was attracted by its secret, I felt closer to him. I told him what I had never told anyone. My childhood, my mystic dreams, my religious passions, my memories of German concentration camps, my belief that I was now just a messenger of the dead among the living. . . .

I talked for hours. He listened, leaning heavily on the railing, without interrupting me, without moving, without taking his eyes off a shadow that followed the ship. From time to time he would light a cigarette and, even when I stopped in the middle of a thought or a sentence, he said nothing.

Sometimes I left a sentence unfinished, jumped from one episode to another, or described a character in a word without mentioning the event with which he was connected. The stranger didn't ask for explanations. At times I spoke very softly, so softly that it was impossible that he heard a word of what I was saying; but he remained motionless and silent. He seemed not to dare exist outside of silence.

Only toward the end of the night did he recover his speech. His voice, a streak of shade, was hoarse. The voice of a man who, alone in the night, looks at the sea, looks at his own death.

"You must know this," he finally said. "I think I'm going to hate you."

Emotion made me gasp. I felt like shaking his hand to thank him. Few people would have had the courage to accompany me lucidly to the end.

The stranger threw his head back as if to make sure that the sky was still there. Suddenly he started hammering the railing with his clenched fist. And in a restrained, deep voice he repeated the same words over and over, "I'm going to hate you . . . I'm going to hate you. . . ."

Then he turned his back to me and walked off.

A fringe of white light was brightening the horizon. The sea was quiet, the ship was dozing. The stars had started to disappear. It was daybreak.

I stayed on deck all day. I came back to the same place the following night. The stranger never joined me again.

"I'll take a chance," Kathleen said.

I got up and took a few steps around the room to stretch my legs. I stopped at the window and looked out. The sidewalk across the street was covered with snow. A strange anguish came over me. Cold sweat covered my forehead. Once again the night would lift its burden and it would be day. I was afraid of the day. At night, I find all faces familiar, every noise sounds like something already heard. During the day, I only run into strangers.

"Do you know what Shimon Yanai told me about you?" Kathleen asked.

"I have no idea."

What could he have told her? What does he know about me? Nothing. He doesn't know that when I get carried away by a sunset, my heart fills with such nostalgia for Sighet, the little town of my childhood, it begins to pound so hard, so fast, that a week later I still haven't caught my breath; he doesn't know that I'm more moved by a Hassidic melody, which brings men back to his origins, than by Bach, Beethoven, and Mozart together; he couldn't know that when I look at a woman, it is always the image of my grandmother that I see.

"Shimon Yanai thinks you're a saint," Kathleen said.

My answer was a loud, unrestrained laugh.

"Shimon Yanai says that you suffered a lot. Only saints suffer a lot."

I couldn't stop laughing. I turned toward Kathleen, toward her eyes, not made for seeing, nor for crying, but for speaking and perhaps for making people laugh. She

47

was hiding her chin in the neck of her sweater, concealing her lips which were trembling.

"Me, a saint? What a joke. . . ."

"Why are you laughing?"

"I'm laughing," I answered still shaking, "I'm laughing because I'm not a saint. Saints don't laugh. Saints are dead. My grandmother was a saint: she's dead. My teacher was a saint: he's dead. But me, look at me, I'm alive. And I'm laughing. I'm alive and I'm laughing because I'm not a saint. . . ."

At first I had had a hard time getting used to the idea that I was alive. I thought of myself as dead. I couldn't eat, read, cry: I saw myself dead. I thought I was dead and that in a dream I imagined myself alive. I knew I no longer existed, that my real self had stayed *there,* that my present self had nothing in common with the other, the real one. I was like the skin shed by a snake.

Then one day, in the street, an old woman asked me to come up to her room. She was so old, so dried out, that I couldn't hold back my laughter. The old woman grew pale and I thought she was going to collapse at my feet.

"Haven't you any pity?" she said in a choked voice.

Then, all of a sudden, reality struck me: I was alive, laughing, making fun of unhappy old women, I was able to humiliate and hurt old women who, like saints, spit on their own bodies.

"Where does suffering lead to?" Kathleen asked tensely. "Not to saintliness?"

"No!" I shouted.

That stopped my laughter. I was getting angry. I walked away from the window and stood in front of her; she was sitting on the floor now, her arms around her knees and her head resting on her arms.

"Those who say that are false prophets," I said.

I had to make an effort not to scream, not to wake up the whole house, and the dead who were waiting outside in the wind and the snow flurries. I went on:

"Suffering brings out the lowest, the most cowardly in man. There is a phase of suffering you reach beyond which you become a brute: beyond it you sell your soul—and worse, the souls of your friends—for a piece of bread, for some warmth, for a moment of oblivion, of sleep. Saints are those who die before the end of the story. The others, those who live out their destiny, no longer dare look at themselves in the mirror, afraid they may see their inner image: a monster laughing at unhappy women and at saints who are dead. . . ."

Kathleen listened, in a daze, her eyes wide open. As I spoke, her back bent over even more. Her pale lips whispered the same sentence tirelessly, "Go on! I want to know more. Go on!"

Then I fell on my knees, took her head in my hands, and, looking straight into her eyes, I told her the story of my grandmother, then the story of my little sister, and of my father, and of my mother; in very simple words, I described to her how man can become a grave for the unburied dead.

I kept talking. In every detail, I described the screams and the nightmares that haunt me at night. And Kathleen, very pale, her eyes, red, continued to beg:

"More! Go on! More!"

She was saying "more" in the eager voice of a woman who wants her pleasure to last, who asks the man she loves not to stop, not to leave her, not to disappoint her, not to abandon her halfway between ecstasy and nothing. "More. . . . More. . . ."

I kept looking at her and holding her. I wanted to get rid of all the filth that was in me and graft it onto her pupils and her lips which were so pure, so innocent, so beautiful.

I bared my soul. My most contemptible thoughts and desires, my most painful betrayals, my vaguest lies, I tore them from inside me and placed them in front of her, like an impure offering, so she could see them and smell their stench.

But Kathleen was drinking in every one of my words as if she wanted to punish herself for not having suffered before. From time to time she insisted in the same eager voice that sounded so much like the old prostitute's, "More. . . . More. . . ."

Finally I stopped, exhausted. I stretched out on the carpet and closed my eyes.

We didn't talk for a long time: an hour, perhaps two. I was out of breath. I was wet with perspiration, my shirt stuck to my body. Kathleen didn't stir. Outside, the night softly moved on.

Suddenly we heard the noise of the milkman's truck, coming from the street. The truck stopped near the door.

Kathleen took a deep breath and said, "I feel like going down and kissing the milkman."

I didn't answer. I didn't have the strength.

"I would like to kiss him," Kathleen said, "just to thank him. To thank him for being alive."

I was silent.

"You're not saying anything." She sounded surprised. "You're not laughing?"

And as I still didn't say anything, she began to stroke my hair, then her fingers explored the outlines of my face. I liked the way she caressed me.

"I like you to touch me," I told her, my eyes still closed. After hesitating, I added, "You see, it's the best proof that I'm not a saint. Saints in that respect are like the dead: they don't know desire."

Kathleen's voice became lighter and sounded more provocative. "And you desire me?"

"Yes."

I again felt like laughing: a saint, me? What a wonderful joke! Me, a saint! Does a saint feel this desire for a woman's body? Does he feel this need to take her into his arms, cover her with kisses, to bite her flesh, to possess her breath, her life, her breasts? No, a saint would not be willing to make love to a woman, with his dead grandmother watching, wearing her black shawl that seems to hold the nights and days of the universe.

I sat down. And I said angrily, "I'm not a saint!"

"No?" Kathleen asked without being able to smile.

"No," I repeated.

I opened my eyes and noticed that she was really suffering. She was biting her lips; there was despair in her face.

"I'll prove to you that I'm not a saint," I muttered angrily.

Without a word I started to undress her. She didn't resist. When she was naked, she sat down again as before. Her head resting on her knees, she looked at me in anguish as I too undressed. Now there were two lines around her mouth. I could see fear in her eyes. I was pleased; she was afraid of me, and that was good. Those who, like me, have left their souls in hell, are here only to frighten others by being their mirrors.

"I am going to take you," I told her in a harsh, almost hostile voice. "But I don't love you."

I thought: she must know. I'm not a saint at all. I'll

make love without any commitments. A saint commits his whole being with every act.

She undid her hair, which fell to her shoulders. Her breast rose and fell irregularly.

"What if I fall in love with you?" she asked with studied naïveté.

"Small chance! You'll hate me rather."

Her face became a little sadder, a little more distressed. "I'm afraid you're right."

Somewhere, above the city, there was a hint of dawn in the foggy world.

"Look at me," I said.

"I'm looking at you."

"What do you see?"

"A saint," she answered.

I laughed again. There we were, both naked, and one of us was a saint? It was grotesque! I took her brutally, trying to hurt her. She bit her lips and didn't cry out. We stayed together until late that afternoon.

Without saying another word.

Without exchanging a kiss.

Suddenly, the fever vanished. My name was taken off the critical list. I still had pain, but my life was no longer in danger. I was still given antibiotics, but less frequently. Four shots a day. Then three, then two. Then none.

When I was allowed visitors, I had been in the hospital for nearly a week and in a cast for three days.

"Your friends may come to see you today," the nurse said as she washed me.

"Fine," I said.

"That's your only reaction? Aren't you pleased to be able to see your friends?"

"I am. Very pleased."

"You've come a long way," she said.

"A very long way."

"You're not talkative."

"No."

I had discovered one advantage in being ill: you can remain silent without having to apologize.

"After breakfast, I'll come and shave you," the nurse said.

"It won't be necessary," I answered.

"Not necessary?"

She seemed not to believe me: nothing that's done in a hospital is unnecessary!

"That's right. Unnecessary. I want to grow a beard."

She stared at me a moment, then gave her verdict.

"No. You need a shave. You look too ill this way."

"But I am ill."

"You are. But if I shave you you'll feel better."

And without giving me time to answer, she continued, "You'll feel like new."

She was young, dark, obstinate. Tall, buttoned up in her white uniform, she towered over me and not merely because she was standing up.

"All right," I said, to put an end to the discussion. "In that case, fine."

"Good! That's the boy!"

She was happy with her victory, her mouth wide open showing her white teeth. Laughingly, she began to tell me all kinds of stories which seemed to have the following moral: death is afraid to attack those who make themselves look nice in the morning. The secret of immortality may well be to find the right shaving cream.

After helping me wash, she brought my breakfast.

"I'll feed you as if you were a baby. Aren't you ashamed to be a baby? At your age?"

She left and immediately returned with an electric razor.

"We want you to look nice. I want my baby to be nice!"

The razor made a tremendous noise. The nurse went on chattering. I wasn't listening to her. I was thinking about the night of the accident. The cab was speeding. I had no idea it would send me to the hospital.

"There you are," the nurse said beaming. "Now you're nice."

"I know," I said. "Now I'm like a newborn baby!"

"Wait and I'll bring you a mirror!"

She had very large eyes, with black pupils, and the white around them was very white.

"I don't want it," I said.

"I'll bring it, you'll see."

"Listen," I said threateningly, "if you hand me a mirror I'll break it. A broken mirror brings seven years of unhappiness! Is that what you want? Seven years of unhappiness?"

For a second her eyes were still, wondering if I wasn't joking.

"It's true. Anybody will tell you: one should never break a mirror."

She was still laughing, but now her voice sounded more worried than before. She was wiping her hands on her white uniform.

"You're a bad boy," she said. "I don't like you."

"Too bad!" I answered. "I adore you!"

She muttered something to herself and left the room.

I was facing the window and could see the East River from my bed. A small boat was going by: a grayish spot on a blue background. A mirage.

Someone knocked at the door.

"Come in!"

Dr. Paul Russel, hands in his pockets, was back to resume our conversation where we had left off.

"Feeling better this morning?"

"Yes, Doctor. Much better."

"No more fever. The enemy is beaten."

"A beaten enemy, that's dangerous," I remarked. "He'll only think of vengeance."

The doctor became more serious. He took out a cigarette and offered it to me. I refused. He lit it for himself.

"Do you still have pain?"

"Yes."

"It will last a few weeks more. You're not afraid?"

"Of what?"

"Of suffering."

"No. I'm not afraid of suffering."

He looked me straight in the eye. "What are you afraid of, then?"

Again I had the impression that he was keeping something from me. Could he actually know? Had I talked in my sleep, during the operation?

"I'm not afraid of anything," I answered, staring back at him.

There was a silence.

He went to the window and stayed there a few moments. There, I thought: the back of a man and the river no longer exists. Paradise is when nothing comes between the eye and the tree.

"You have a beautiful view," he said without turning.

"Very beautiful. The river is like me: it hardly moves."

"Sheer illusion! It is calm only on the surface. Go beneath the surface, you'll see how restless it is. . . ." He turned suddenly. ". . . Just like you, as a matter of fact."

What does he know exactly, I wondered, somewhat worried. He speaks as if he knows. Is it possible that I betrayed myself?

"Every man is like the river," I said to shift the conversation toward abstractions. "Rivers flow toward the sea, which is never full. Men are swallowed up by death which is never satiated."

He made a gesture of discouragement, as if to say, All right, you don't want to talk, you're dodging, it doesn't matter. I'll wait.

Slowly he moved toward the door, then stopped.

"I have a message for you. From Kathleen. She's coming to see you in the late afternoon."

"You saw her?"

"Yes. She's been coming every day. She's an extremely nice girl."

"Ex-treme-ly."

He was standing in the opening of the door. His voice seemed very close. The door must have been right next to my bed.

"She loves you," he said. His voice became hard, insistent. "And you? Do you love her?"

He stressed the "you." I was breathing faster. What does he know, I asked myself, tormented.

"Of course," I answered, trying to look calm. "Of course I love her."

Nothing stirred. There was complete silence. In the hallway, the foggy loud speaker announced: "Dr. Braunstein, telephone . . . Dr. Braunstein, telephone . . ." Echoes from another world. In the room there was utter silence.

"Fine," Dr. Russel said. "I have to go. I'll see you tonight, or tomorrow."

Another boat was gliding by the window. Outside the air was sharp, alive. I thought: at this very moment, men are walking in the streets, without ties, in their shirt sleeves. They are reading, arguing, eating, drinking, stopping to avoid a car, to admire a woman, to look at windows. Outside, at this very moment, men are walking.

Toward the beginning of the afternoon, some of my colleagues showed up. They came together, gay and trying to make me feel equally gay.

They told me some gossip: who was doing what, who was saying what, who was unfaithful to whom. The latest word, the latest indiscretion, the latest story.

Then the conversation came back to the accident.

"You must admit you've been lucky: this could have been it," one of them said.

And another: "Or you could have lost a leg."

"Or even your mind."

"You're going to be rich," Sandor, a Hungarian, said. "I was hit by a car once myself. I got a thousand dollars from the insurance company. You were lucky it was a cab. Cabs always have a lot of insurance. You'll be rich, you'll see, you lucky bastard!"

I hurt everywhere. I couldn't move. I was practically paralyzed. But I was very lucky. I was going to be rich. I'd be able to travel, go to night clubs, keep mistresses, be on top of the world: what luck! They just about said they envied me.

"I'd always been told that in America you find dollars in the street," I said. "So it's true: you just have to fall down to pick them up."

They laughed still more and I laughed with them. Once or twice the nurse came in to bring me something to drink and she also laughed with them.

"And you know this morning he didn't even want to shave!" she told them.

58

"He's rich," Sandor said. "Rich men can afford to be unshaven."

"You're funny," the nurse exclaimed, clapping her hands. "And did he tell you about the mirror?"

"No!" they all shouted together. "Tell us about the mirror!"

She told them that I had refused to look at myself in the mirror that morning.

"Rich men are afraid of mirrors," I said. "Mirrors have no respect for that which glitters. They're too familiar with it."

It was warm in the room, even warmer than in the cast. My friends were perspiring. The nurse was wiping her forehead with the back of her hand. When she left, Sandor winked.

"Not bad, hum?"

"She must be something!" another added.

"Well, you won't get bored here, you can be sure of that much!"

"No, I won't get bored," I said.

We had been together for quite some time, when Sandor remembered that there was a press conference at four.

"That's true, we'd forgotten."

They left in a hurry, taking their laughter with them into the hallway, into the street, and finally, where it assumes an historic function, into the United Nations Building.

It was nearly seven when Kathleen arrived. She seemed paler than usual, and gayer, also more exuberant. It was as if she were living the happiest moments of her life. What a beautiful view! Look, the river! And such a nice room! So big, so clean! You're looking great!

It's weird, I thought. A hospital room is the gayest place on earth. Everybody turns into an actor. Even the patients. You put on new attitudes, new make-up, new joys.

Kathleen kept talking. Even though she didn't like people who talk without saying anything, she was doing precisely that now. Why is she afraid of silence? I wondered, as I grew more tense. Is it possible she knows something too? She is in a position to know. She was there at the time of the accident. A little ahead. She may have turned around.

I would have liked to steer the conversation to that subject, but I couldn't stop the flow of her words. She kept talking and talking. Isak is replacing you on the paper. In the office, the phone keeps ringing: all kinds of people asking how you are. And you know, even the one—what's his name?—you know the one I mean, the fat one, the one who looks pregnant, you know, the one who's angry at you, even he called. Isak told me. And——

There was a knock on the door. A nurse—a new one, not the morning nurse—brought in my dinner. She was an old woman with glasses, haughtily indifferent. She offered to help me eat.

"Don't bother," Kathleen said. "I'll do it."

"Very well," the old nurse said. "As you wish."

I wasn't hungry. Kathleen kept insisting: some soup? Yes, yes. You have to. You've lost a lot of strength. Come on. Just one spoonful. Just one. One more. Do it for me. And one more. Fine. And now the rest. Let's see: a piece of meat. Ah! Does that look good!

I closed my eyes and tried not to hear. That was the only way. I suddenly felt like shouting. But I knew I shouldn't. Anyway what would have been the use?

Kathleen talked on and on.

". . . I also retained a lawyer. A very good one. He's going to sue the cab company. He'll be here tomorrow. He is very hopeful. He says you'll get a lot of money. . . ."

When I was through eating, she took the tray and put it on the table. I could see as she busied herself how tired she was. Now I understood why she was talking so much: she was at the end of her strength. Behind her forced good-humor was exhaustion. Seven days. It had been a week since the accident.

"Kathleen?" I called.

"Yes?"

"Come here. Sit down."

She obeyed and sat on the bed.

"What is it?" she asked worried.

"I want to ask you something."

She frowned. "Yes?"

"I don't recognize you. You've changed. You talk a lot. Why?"

A shudder went through her eyelids, through her shoulders.

"So many things have happened in a week," she said blushing slightly. "I want to tell you about them. Everything. Don't forget that I haven't talked to you in a week. . . ."

She looked at me as if she had been beaten, and lowered her head. Then slowly, mechanically, she repeated several times in a low, tired, toneless voice, "I don't want to cry, I don't want to cry, I don't want to. . . ."

Poor Kathleen, I thought. Poor Kathleen. I have changed her. Kathleen so proud, Kathleen whose will was stronger than others', Kathleen whose strength was pure and who was truly tough, Kathleen against whom men with character, strong-minded men, liked to pit themselves; now Kathleen didn't even have the strength to hold back her tears, her words.

I had transformed her. And she had wanted to change me! "You can't change a human being," I had told her in the beginning, once, a thousand times. "You can change someone's thoughts, someone's attitudes, someone's ties. You might even change someone's desires, but that's all." "That's enough for me," she had answered.

And the battle had started. She wanted to make me happy no matter what. To make me taste the pleasures of life. To make me forget the past. "Your past is dead. Dead and buried," she would say. And I would answer, "I am my past. If it's buried, I'm buried with it."

She was fighting stubbornly. "I'm strong," she would say. "I'll win." And I would answer, "You are strong. You are beautiful. You have all the qualities to conquer the living. But here you are fighting the dead. You cannot conquer the dead!" "We shall see."

"I don't want to cry," she said, her head down, as if under the weight of all the dead since creation.

I had said human beings don't change? I was wrong. They do. The dead are all-powerful. That's what she refused to understand: that the dead are invincible. That through me she was fighting them.

The only child of very rich parents, she was determined and obstinate. Her arrogance was almost naïve. She wasn't accustomed to losing battles. She thought she could take the place of my fate.

Once I had asked her if she loved me. "No," she had answered heatedly. And it was true. She hadn't lied. The truly proud don't lie.

Our understanding had nothing to do with love. Not at first. Later, yes. But not at the beginning. What united us was exactly what kept us apart. She liked life and love; I only thought of life and love with a strong feeling of shame. We stayed together. She needed to fight and I was watching her. I watched her knocking against the cold, unchanging reality she had discovered first in my words, then in my silence.

We traveled a lot. The days were full, the hours dense. Time was once more an adventure. Whenever Kathleen watched a beautiful dawn, she knew how to make me share her enthusiasm; in the street she was the one to point out beautiful women; at home she taught me that the body is also a source of joy.

At first, at the very beginning, I avoided her kisses. We were living together but our mouths had never met. Something in me shrank from the touch of her lips. It was as if I were afraid that she would become different if I kissed her. Several times she had nearly asked me why but she had been too proud. Then, little by little, I let myself go. Every kiss reopened an old wound. And I was aware that I was still capable of suffering. That I was still answering the calls of the past.

Our affair lasted a whole year. When we celebrated the first anniversary of our meeting—that's what we liked to call our affair—we both decided to separate. Since the experiment had foundered, there was no reason to draw it out.

That night neither one of us slept. Stretched out next to each other, frightened, in silence, we waited for daybreak. Just before dawn, she pulled me toward her and in the dark our bodies made love for the last time. An hour later, still silent, I got up, dressed, and left the room without saying good-bye, without even turning around.

Outside, the biting morning wind whipped the houses. The streets were still deserted. Somewhere a door creaked. A window lit up, lonely and pale. It was cold. My legs would have liked me to run. I managed to walk slowly, very slowly: I didn't want to give in to any weakness. My eyes were crying, probably because of the cold.

"I don't want to cry," Kathleen said.

She was shaking her lowered head.

Poor Kathleen, I thought. You too have been changed by the dead.

The lawyer came the next day. He wore glasses, was of medium height, and had the self-satisfied air of someone who knows the answer before he has even asked you the question.

He introduced himself: Mark Brown. "Call me Mark."

He sat down as if he were at home and took a large yellow pad out of his brief case.

"I talked to your doctors," he said. "You were in very bad shape. That's very good."

"You're right, that's very good."

He understood the irony. "Of course I'm only speaking from the point of view of the lawsuit," he said, winking at me.

"So am I," I answered. "I hear you're going to make me rich."

"I have high hopes."

"Be careful. My enemies will never forgive me: I'm about to become a rich journalist!"

He laughed: "For once the law will be on the side of literature!"

64

He started asking me detailed questions: what exactly had happened on the night of the accident? Had I been alone? No. Who was with me? Kathleen. Yes, the young woman who had called him. Had we quarreled? No. Had we waited for the light to turn green before crossing the street? Yes. The cab had come from the left. Had I seen it approaching?

I took a little more time to answer this last question. Mark took off his glasses and as he wiped them he repeated, "Did you see it approaching?"

"No," I said.

He looked at me more sharply. "You seem to hesitate."

"I'm trying to relive the incident, to see it again."

Mark was intelligent, perceptive. To prepare a good case, he was determined to get lots of details which, on the surface, seemed to have no direct relation to the accident. Before working out his strategy he wanted to know everything. His questioning lasted several hours. He seemed satisfied.

"Not the shadow of a doubt," he decided. "The driver is guilty of negligence."

"I hope he won't have to suffer because of this!" I said. "I wouldn't want him to be punished. After all he didn't do it on purpose. . . ."

"Don't worry," he reassured me, "he won't have to pay; it will be the insurance company. We have nothing against him, poor chap."

"You're sure, absolutely sure, that nothing will happen to him?"

Poor devil, I thought. It wasn't his fault. The day before, his wife had called and asked me to forgive him. She was calling on behalf of her husband. He was afraid. He was even afraid to ask me to forgive him.

"Absolutely sure," the lawyer said with a little, dry laugh. "You'll be richer and he won't be any poorer. So, there's nothing to worry about."

I couldn't hide a sigh of relief.

Every morning Dr. Russel came to chat. He had made it a habit to end his daily rounds with me. Often he would remain an hour or more. He would walk in without knocking, sit on the window sill, his hands in the pockets of his white coat, his legs crossed, his eyes reflecting the changing colors of the river.

He spoke a lot about himself, his life in the army—he had been in the Korean War—his work, the pleasures and disappointments that came with it. Each prey torn away from death made him as happy as if he had won a universal victory. A defeat left dark rings under his eyes. I only had to look at him carefully to know whether the night before he had won or lost the battle. He considered death his personal enemy.

"What makes me despair," he often told me bitterly, "is that our weapons aren't equal. My victories can only be temporary. My defeats are final. Always."

One morning he seemed happier than usual. He gave up his favorite spot near the window and started walking up and down the room like a drunkard, talking to himself.

"You have been drinking, Doctor!" I teased him.

"Drinking!" he exclaimed. "Of course I haven't been drinking. I don't drink. Today I'm simply happy. Awfully happy. I won! Yes, this time I won. . . ."

His victory tasted like wine. He couldn't stand still. To split up his happiness he would have liked to be simultaneously himself and someone else: witness and hero. He wanted to sing and to hear himself singing, to dance and to

66

see himself dancing, to climb to the top of the highest mountain and to shout, to scream with all his strength, "I won! I conquered Death!"

The operation had been difficult, dangerous: a little twelve-year-old boy who had a very slim chance of surviving. Three doctors had given up hope. But he, Paul Russel, had decided to try the impossible.

"The kid will make it!" he thundered, his face glowing as if lit up by a sun inside him. "Do you understand? He's going to live! And yet all seemed lost! The infection had reached his leg and was poisoning his blood. I amputated the leg. The others were saying that it wouldn't do any good. That it was too late. That the game was lost. But I didn't hesitate. I started to act. For each breath, I had to fight with every weapon I had. But you see: I won! This time I really won!"

The joy of saving a human life, I thought. I have never experienced it. I didn't even know that it existed. To hold in your hands a boy's life is to take God's place. I had never dreamt of rising above the level of man. Man is not defined by what denies him, but by that which affirms him. This is found within, not across from him or next to him.

"You see," Paul Russel said in a different tone of voice, "the difference between you and me is this. Your relation with what surrounds you and with what marks the limits of your horizon develops in an indirect way. You only know the words, the skin, the appearances, the ideas, of life. There'll always be a curtain between you and your neighbor's life. You're not content to know man is alive; you also want to know what he is doing with his life. For me this is different. I am less severe with my fellow men. We have the same enemy and it has only one name: Death. Before it we are all equal. In its eyes no life has more weight than another. From that point of view, I am just like Death. What fascinates me in man is his capacity for living. Acts are just repetitions. If you had ever held a man's life in the palm of your hand, you too would come to prefer the immediate to the future, the concrete to the ideal, and life to the problems which it brings with it."

He stood at the window for a moment and stopped talking, just long enough to smile, before continuing an octave lower.

"Your life, my friend, I had it right there. In the palm of my hand."

He turned slowly, his hand held out. Little by little his face became as it usually was and his gestures became less abrupt.

"Do you believe in God, Doctor?"

My question took him by surprise. He stopped suddenly, wrinkling his forehead.

"Yes," he answered. "But not in the operating room. There I only count on myself."

His eyes looked deeper. He added, "On myself and on the patient. Or, if you prefer, on the life in the diseased flesh. Life wants to live. Life wants to go on. It is opposed to death. It fights. The patient is my ally. He fights on my side. Together we are stronger than the enemy. Take the boy last night. He didn't accept death. He helped me to win the battle. He was holding on, clinging. He was asleep, anesthetized, and yet he was taking part in the fight. . . ."

Still motionless, he again stared at me intensely. There was an awkward silence. Once more I had the impression he knew, that he was speaking only to penetrate my secret. Now, I decided. Now or never. I had to put an end to any uncertainty.

"Doctor, I would like to ask you a question."

He nodded.

"What did I say during the operation?"

He thought a moment. "Nothing. You didn't say any-thing."

"Are you sure? Not even a word?"

"Not even a word."

I was relieved and couldn't help smiling.

"My turn now," the doctor said seriously. "I also have a question."

My smile froze. "Go ahead," I said.

I had to fight an urge to close my eyes. All of a sudden the room seemed too light. Anxiety took hold of my voice, my breath, my eyes.

The doctor lowered his head slightly, almost imper-ceptibly.

"Why don't you care about living?" he asked very softly.

For a moment everything shook. Even the light flickered and changed color. It was white, red, black. The blood was beating in my temples. My head was no longer my own.

"Don't deny it," the doctor went on, speaking still more softly. "Don't deny it. I know."

He knows. He knows. He knows. My throat was in an invisible vise. I was going to choke any moment.

Weakly I asked him who had told him: Kathleen?

"No. Not Kathleen. Nobody. Nobody told me. But I know it anyway. I guessed. During the operation. You never helped me. Not once. You abandoned me. I had to wage the fight alone, all alone. Worse. You were on the other side, against me, on the side of the enemy."

His voice became hard, painfully hard. "Answer me! Why don't you want to live? Why?"

I was calm again. He doesn't know, I thought. The little he is guessing is nothing. An impression. That's all. Nothing definite. Nothing worked out. And yet he is moving in the right direction. Only he's not going all the way.

"Answer me," he repeated. "Why? Why?"

He was becoming more and more insistent. His lower lip was shaking nervously. Was he aware of it? I thought: he's angry at me because I left him alone, because even now I escape him and have neither gratitude nor admiration for him. That's why he's angry. He guessed that I don't care about living, that deep inside me there is no desire left to go on. And that undermines the foundation of his philosophy and his system of values. Man, according to his book, must live and must fight for his life. He must help doctors and not fight them. I had fought him. He brought me back to life against my will. I had nearly joined my grandmother. I was actually on the threshold. Paul Russel stood behind me and prevented me from crossing. He was pulling me toward him. Alone against Grandmother and the others. And he had won. Another victory for him. A human life. I should shout with happiness and make the walls of the universe tremble. But instead I disturb him. That's what is distressing him.

Dr. Russel was making an obvious effort to restrain himself. He was still looking at me with anger, his cheeks purple, his lips trembling.

"I order you to answer me!"

A pitiless inquisitor, he had raised his voice. A cold anger made his hands rigid.

I thought: he is going to shout, to hit me. Who knows? He might be capable of strangling me, of sending me back to the battlefield. Dr. Russel is a human being, therefore capable of hatred, capable of losing control. He could easily put his hands around my neck and squeeze. That would be normal, logical on his part. I represent a danger to him. Anyone who rejects life is a threat to him and to everything he stands for in this world where life already counts for so little. In his eyes I am a cancer to be eliminated. What would become of humanity and of the laws of equilibrium if all men began to desire death?

I felt very calm, completely controlled. If I had searched further I might have discovered that my calm also hid the satisfaction, the strange joy—or was it simply humor?—that comes from the knowledge of one's own strength, of one's own solitude. I was telling myself: he doesn't know. And I alone can decide to tell him, to transform his future. At this very moment, I am his fate.

"Did I tell you the dream I had during the first operation I ever had?" I asked him smilingly in an amused tone of voice. "No? Shall I tell you? I was twelve. My mother had taken me to a clinic that belonged to my cousin, the surgeon Oscar Sreter, to have my tonsils removed. He had put me to sleep with ether. When I woke up, Oscar Sreter asked me, 'Are you crying because it hurts?' 'No,' I answered. 'I'm crying because I just saw God.' Strange dream. I had gone to heaven. God, sitting on his throne, was presiding over an assembly of angels. The distance which separated Him from me was infinite but I could see Him as clearly as if He had been right next to me. God motioned to me and I started to walk forward. I walked several lifetimes but the distance grew no shorter. Then two angels picked me up, and suddenly I found myself face to face with God. At last! I thought. Now I can ask Him the question that haunts all the wise men of Israel: What is the meaning of suffering? But, awed, I couldn't utter a sound. In the meantime other questions kept moving through my head: When will the hour of deliverance come? When will Good conquer Evil, thus allowing chaos to be forever dispelled? But my lips could only tremble and the words stuck in my throat. Then God talked to me. The silence had become so total, so pure, that my heart was ashamed of its beating. The silence was still as absolute, when I heard the words of God. With Him the word and the silence were not contradictory. God answered all my questions and many others. Then two angels took me by the arm again and brought me back. One of them told the other, 'He has become heavier,' and the other replied, 'He is carrying an important answer.' That is when I woke up. Dr. Sreter was leaning over me with a smile. I wanted to tell him that I had just heard the words of God, when I realized to my horror that I had forgotten them. I no longer knew what God had told me. My tears began to flow. 'Are you crying because it hurts?' the good Dr. Sreter asked me. 'It doesn't hurt,' I answered. 'I'm crying because I just saw God. He talked to me and I forgot what He said.' The doctor burst into a friendly laugh: 'If you want I can put you back to sleep; and you can ask Him to repeat. . . .' I was crying and my cousin was laughing heartily. . . . And you see, Doctor, this time, stretched out on your operating table, fast asleep, I didn't see God in my dream. He was no longer there."

Paul Russel had been listening attentively. Leaning forward he seemed to be looking for a hidden meaning in every word. His face had changed.

"You haven't answered my question!" he remarked, still tense.

So he hadn't understood. An answer to his question? But this was an answer! Couldn't he see how the second operation was different from the first? It wasn't his fault. He couldn't understand. We were so different, so far from each other. His fingers touched life. Mine death. Without

72

an intermediary, without partitions. Life, death, each as bare, as true as the other. The problem went beyond us. It was in an invisible sphere, on a faraway screen, between two powers for whom we were only ambassadors.

Standing in front of my bed, he filled the room with his presence. He was waiting. He suspected a secret that made him angry. That's what was throwing him off. We were both young, and above all we were alive. He looked at me steadily, stubbornly, to catch in me that which eluded him. In the same way primitive man must have watched the day disappear behind the mountain.

I felt like telling him: go. Paul Russel, you are a straightforward and courageous man. Your duty is to leave me. Don't ask me to talk. Don't try to know. Neither who I am, nor who you are. I am a storyteller. My legends can only be told at dusk. Whoever listens questions his life. Go, Paul Russel. Go. The heroes of my legends are cruel and without pity. They are capable of strangling you. You want to know who I am, truly? I don't know myself. Sometimes I am Shmuel, the slaughterer. Look at me carefully. No, not at my face. At my hands.

They were about ten in the bunker. Night after night they could hear the German police dogs looking through the ruins for Jews hiding out in their underground shelters. Shmuel and the others were living on practically no water or bread, on hardly any air. They were holding out. They knew that there, down below in their narrow jail, they were free; above, death was waiting for them. One night a disaster nearly occurred. It was Golda's fault. She had taken her child with her. A baby, a few months old. He began to cry, thus endangering the lives of all. Golda was trying to quiet him, to make him sleep. To no avail.

73

That's when the others, including Golda herself, turned to Shmuel and told him: "Make him shut up. Take care of him, you whose job it is to slaughter chickens. You will be able to do it without making him suffer too much." And Shmuel gave in to reason: the baby's life in exchange for the lives of all. He had taken the child. In the dark his groping fingers felt for the neck. And there had been silence on earth and in heaven. There was only the sound of dogs barking in the distance.

A slight smile came to my lips. Shmuel too had been a doctor, I thought.

Motionless, Paul Russel was still waiting.

Moishe is a smuggler. He too comes from Sighet. We were friends. Every morning at six, ever since we were eight years old, we met in the street and, lantern in hand, we walked to the *cheder* where we found books bigger than we. Moishe wanted to become a rabbi. Today he is a smuggler and he is wanted by every police force in Europe. In the concentration camp he had seen a pious man exchange his whole week's bread rations for a prayer book. The pious man passed away less than a month later. Before dying he had kissed his precious book and murmured, "Book, how many human beings have you destroyed?" That day Moishe had decided to change the course of his existence. And that's how the human race gained a smuggler and lost a rabbi. And it isn't any the worse off for it.

You want to know who I am, Doctor? I am also Moishe the smuggler. But above all I am the one who saw his grandmother go to heaven. Like a flame, she chased away the sun and took its place. And this new sun which blinds

74

instead of giving light forces me to walk with my head down. It weighs upon the future of man. It casts a gloom over the hearts and vision of generations to come.

If I had spoken to him out loud, he would have understood the tragic fate of those who came back, left over, living-dead. You must look at them carefully. Their appearance is deceptive. They are smugglers. They look like the others. They eat, they laugh, they love. They seek money, fame, love. Like the others. But it isn't true: they are playing, sometimes without even knowing it. Anyone who has seen what they have seen cannot be like the others, cannot laugh, love, pray, bargain, suffer, have fun, or forget. Like the others. You have to watch them carefully when they pass by an innocent looking smokestack, or when they lift a piece of bread to their mouths. Something in them shudders and makes you turn your eyes away. These people have been amputated; they haven't lost their legs or eyes but their will and their taste for life. The things they have seen will come to the surface again sooner or later. And then the world will be frightened and won't dare look these spiritual cripples in the eye.

If I had spoken out loud, Paul Russel would have understood why one shouldn't ask those who came back too many questions: they aren't normal human beings. A spring snapped inside them from the shock. Sooner or later the results must appear. But I didn't want him to understand. I didn't want him to lose his equilibrium; I didn't want him to see a truth which threatened to reveal itself at any moment.

I began to persuade him he was wrong so he would go away, so he would leave me alone. Of course I wanted to live. Obviously I wanted to live, create, do lasting things, help man make a step forward, contribute to the progress of humanity, its happiness, its fulfillment! I talked a long time, passionately, using complicated, grandiloquent words and abstract expressions on purpose. And since he still wasn't completely convinced, I threw in the argument to which he couldn't remain deaf: love. I love Kathleen. I love her with all my heart. And how can one love if at the same time one doesn't care about life, if one doesn't believe in life or in love?

The young doctor's face gradually assumed its usual expression. He had heard the words he wanted to hear. His philosophy wasn't threatened. Everything was in order again. Nothing like friendship between patients and doctors! Nothing is more sacred than life, or healthier, or greater, or more noble. To refuse life is a sin; it's stupid and mad. You have to accept life, cherish it, love it, fight for it as if it were a treasure, a woman, a secret happiness.

Now he was becoming friendly again. He offered me a cigarette, encouraging me to accept it. He was no longer tense. His lips had their normal color again. There was no more anger in his eyes.

"I'm glad," he said finally. "At the beginning I was afraid. . . . I admit my mistake. I'm glad. Really."

I too. I was glad to have convinced him. Really.

Nothing easier. He only wanted to be deceived and I had played his game. I had recited a text he knew by heart. Love is a question mark, not an exclamation point. It can explain everything without calling on arguments whose strength as well as whose weakness is based on logic. A boy who is in love knows more about the universe and about creation than a scholar. Why do we have to die? Because I love you, my love. And why do parallel lines meet at infinity? What a question! It's only because I love you, my love.

And it works. For them, for the boy and for the girl, prisoners of a magic circle, the answer seems completely valid. In their eyes there is a direct relation between their adventure and the mysteries of the universe.

Yes, it was easy. I love Kathleen. Therefore life has a meaning, man isn't alone. Love is the very proof of God's existence.

Kathleen. In the end I managed to convince her also. True, this was more difficult. She knew me better and was on her guard. Unlike the young doctor, who was running away from uncertainties, she had a feeling for nuances. For her, Hamlet was just romantic and the question he asked himself was too simplistic. The problem is not: to be or not to be. But rather: to be and not to be. What it comes down to is that man lives while dying, that he represents death to the living, and that's where tragedy begins.

Why had she come back? She shouldn't have. I had even told her so. No. I hadn't told her. She was unhappy. This had surprised me so much that I had felt incapable of telling her not to reopen the parentheses.

She was suffering. Even on the telephone, her voice had betrayed her weariness. Five years had gone by since my silent departure. It had been bitingly cold that morning. Now it was fall. Five years! I had heard from Shimon Yanai that Kathleen had gone back to Boston and had married a man much older than she, and quite rich.

One afternoon, in the office. Up to my neck in work: the General Assembly of the United Nations was holding its annual session. Speeches, statements, accusations and counteraccusations, resolutions and counterresolutions.

Judging from what was said on the speaker's platform, our planet was extremely ill.

The phone rang.

At the other end, in a whisper, a voice murmured, "It's Kathleen."

That's all she said and there was a long silence. I looked at the receiver I was holding in my hand and I had the impression it was alive. I thought: years ago, winter; now, fall.

"I would like to see you," Kathleen added.

Her voice had the sound of despair. Of nothingness.

"Where are you?" I asked her.

She mentioned a hotel.

"Wait for me," I said.

We hung up at the same time.

She was staying at one of the most expensive and most elegant places in New York. Her apartment was on the fifteenth floor. Quietly I pushed the half-open door. Kathleen was framed by the window. Her beautiful black hair fell to her shoulders. She was wearing a dark gray dress with a low-cut back. I was moved.

"Hello, Kathleen," I said as I walked in.

"Hello," she answered without turning.

I walked toward the open window. It looked on Central Park, the no man's land which at night, in this enormous city, shelters with equal kindness criminals and lovers. The trees were turning orange. It was humid and hot: the last heat wave before winter. Far below, thousands of cars drove into the foliage and disappeared. The sun grafted its golden rays onto the skyscrapers' windows.

"Help me," Kathleen said, her eyes fixed on the dead leaves that covered the park.

Furtively I looked at her left profile. From the curve of

her neck I could see that she was still sensitive.

"You will help me, won't you?" she said.

"Of course," I answered.

Only then did she turn her face toward me, with a look of gratitude. She was still beautiful, but her beauty had lost its pride.

"I've suffered a lot," she said.

"Don't say anything," I answered. "Let me look at you."

I sat down in an armchair and she began to walk about the room. When she talked, a line of sadness appeared near her upper lip. From time to time her eyes had the hard expression that comes from humiliation. She was smoking more than she used to. I thought: Kathleen the proud, Kathleen the untamable, Kathleen the queen—here she is. A beaten woman. A drowning woman.

She sat in the armchair opposite me. She was breathing heavily.

"I want to talk," she said.

"Go ahead," I told her.

"I'm not ashamed to tell you that I want to talk."

"Go ahead," I told her.

"I am no longer ashamed to tell you that I suffered a lot."

"Go ahead, talk."

She was trying to live up to the image she still had of herself. She used to speak firmly and with harsh words. She never used to speak of her own suffering. Now she did. You just had to listen to her and look at her closely to realize that her beauty had lost its power and its mystery.

She spoke for a long time. Sometimes her eyes would cloud over. But she managed not to cry, and I was grateful.

She had gotten married. He loved her. She didn't love him. She did not even love the feeling she had inspired in him. She had agreed to marry him precisely because she did not care about him. What she wanted was to suffer, to pay. Finally her husband understood: Kathleen saw in him not a companion but a kind of judge. She didn't expect happiness from him, however limited, but punishment. That's why he also began to suffer. Their life became a torture chamber. Each was the tormentor and victim of the other. This went on for three years. Then, one day, her husband had had enough. He asked for a divorce. She came to New York. To rest, to find herself again, to see me.

"You'll help me, won't you?"

"Of course," I answered.

All she asked was to stay beside me. Her life was empty. She was hoping to climb up again. To start living again, intensely, as before. To be moved to tears by a transparent dusk, to laugh aloud in the theatre, to protest against ugliness. All she wanted was to become once more what she had been.

I should have refused. I know. Kathleen—the one I had known—deserved more than my consent. To help her was to insult her, to humiliate her. But I accepted. She was unhappy and I was too weak, perhaps too cowardly, to say no to a woman who was hitting her head against a wall, even if this woman was Kathleen.

"Of course," I repeated. "I'll help you."

She moved forward, as if to throw herself into my arms, but held herself back. We looked at each other in silence for a long time.

Who is Sarah?"

I was speechless. Sitting on the edge of the bed, Kathleen watched me with a smile. Her eyes didn't accuse me, they just looked curious.

"You spoke her name the first day, when you were in a coma. You said nothing else. Sarah."

"Why did you wait until today to ask me?"

I had been in the hospital for four weeks.

"I was too curious. I wanted to prove to myself that I was able to wait."

"That's all I said?"

"That's all."

"You're sure?"

"I'm sure. The first few days I was never very far away. You said nothing else. You didn't unclench your teeth. But once or twice you spoke that name: Sarah."

An old suffering stirred somewhere. I didn't know exactly where.

"Sarah," I said distractedly.

Kathleen kept smiling. Her eyes showed no worry. But anguish was there, around her swollen mouth, waiting for a chance to invade her whole face, her whole being.

"Who is she?" she asked again.

"Sarah was my mother's name," I said.

The smile disappeared. Naked suffering was now mixed with the anguish. Kathleen was hardly breathing.

I told her: as a child I lived with the perpetual fear of forgetting my mother's name after I died. In school my teacher had told me: three days after your funeral, an angel will come and knock three times on your grave. He'll ask you your name. You will answer. "I am Eliezer, the son of Sarah." Woe if you forget! A dead soul, you will remain buried for all eternity. You won't be able to come before the tribunal to know if your place is in paradise or in hell with those who waited too long before repenting. You will be condemned to wander in the sphere of chaos where nothing exists, neither punishment nor pain, neither justice nor injustice, neither past nor future, neither hope nor despair. It is a serious thing to forget your mother's name. It is like forgetting your own origin. Remember: "Eliezer, the son of Sarah, the son of Sarah, Sarah, Sarah. . . ."

"Sarah was my mother's name," I said. "I didn't forget it."

Kathleen's body twisted as if she were tied to an invisible stake. She was afraid not to suffer enough. But then she shouldn't have used the state I was in to interpret my silences, to gather names that I had kept secret. My mother's name was Sarah. I never talked about it. I loved her but I had never told her. I loved her with such violence that I had to seem hard toward her so she wouldn't

82

guess. Yes. She is dead. She went to heaven at the side of my grandmother.

"Sarah," Kathleen said in a broken voice. "I like that name. It sounds like Biblical times."

"My mother's name was Sarah," I said again. "She is dead."

Kathleen's face was twisted with pain. She looked like a sorceress who has lost her true face from having put on too many masks. A great fire burned around her. Suddenly she cried out and began to sob. My mother, I had never seen my mother cry.

Sarah.

It was also the name of a girl with blue eyes and golden hair whom I had met in Paris long before I knew Kathleen.

I was reading a newspaper in front of a café near Montparnasse. She was drinking lemonade at the table next to mine. She was trying to attract my attention and this made me blush. She noticed it and smiled.

Embarrassed, I didn't know what attitude to adopt. Where to hide my head, my hands, where to hide my confusion. Finally, unable to stand it any more, I spoke to her.

"You know me?"

"No," she said shaking her head.

"Do I know you?"

"I don't think so," she said teasingly.

I couldn't help stuttering, "Then . . . why? Why . . . why are you staring at me like that?"

She seemed about to shudder, to laugh, or to sigh. "Just like that," she answered.

While cursing my own bashfulness, I buried myself in the newspaper, trying to forget the blond girl and to avoid her straightforward, innocent eyes and the sadness of her smile. The print danced before my eyes. The words didn't stay still long enough for me to catch them. I was going to call the waiter in order to pay and leave, when the girl with the strange smile began to talk to me.

"You're waiting for someone?"

"No," I said.

"I'm not either."

And as she said this, she came over to my table with her glass of lemonade.

"You're alone?" she asked me.

"No," I said blushing still more.

"You don't feel alone?"

"Not at all."

"Really?"

She did not seem to believe me. And her smile was there, like a third presence, somewhere on her face. In her eyes? No. Her eyes were cold, frightened. On her lips? Not there either. They were sensuous, bitter, tired. Where was it then? There, between her forehead and her chin, but I couldn't tell exactly where.

"Really?" she repeated. "You don't feel alone?"

"No."

"How do you manage?"

I was losing face.

"I don't know," I blurted out. "I don't know. I read a lot."

She took a sip, raised her head, and began to laugh at me

openly. I had noticed that in the meantime her real smile had vanished. Maybe she had swallowed it.

"Do you want to make love?" she asked in the same tone of voice.

"Now?" I exclaimed with surprise. "In the afternoon?"

In my mind, love-making was a thing of the night. To make love during the day seemed to me like getting undressed in the middle of the street.

"Right away," she answered. "Do you want to?"

"No," I said quickly.

"Why not?"

"I . . . I don't have any money."

She stared at me a minute with the mocking and forgiving attitude of someone who knows and forgives all.

"That doesn't matter," she said after a pause. "You'll pay me some other time."

I was ashamed. I was afraid. I was young, without any experience. I was afraid not to know what to do. And mostly, I was afraid of afterwards: I would never be the same any more.

"Well? You want to?"

A lock of hair was falling on her forehead. Again the smile appeared. Now I no longer knew if it was the first smile or the one it replaced, the true or the false one.

"Yes," I answered. "I want to."

I thought: this girl has, without knowing it, perhaps, the most elusive smile I have ever seen. I might be able to capture it while making love to her.

"Call the waiter," she said.

I called him. I paid for my coffee; she paid for her lemonade. We got up and began to walk. I felt awkward, ill at ease. Smaller than I, she walked on my right; her head only came a little above my shoulders. I didn't dare look at her.

She lived not far away. The hotel doorman seemed to be sleeping. The girl took her key and told me it was on the third floor. I followed her. From the back she looked less young.

When we got to the third floor, we turned right and went into her room. She told me to close the door. I closed it softly; I didn't want it to make any noise.

"Not like that," the girl said. "Lock it."

I turned the key. I was filled with a new kind of anxiety. I didn't talk as I was sure my voice would tremble. Alone with a woman. Alone in a hotel room with a woman. With a prostitute. And soon we would make love. For I was sure of it: she was a prostitute. Otherwise she would have acted differently.

I was alone with her in her neat and clean room, most of which was painted gray. My first woman would be a prostitute. A prostitute whose strange smile was the smile of a saint.

She had drawn the shades, taken off her shoes, and was waiting. Standing near the bed, she was waiting. I felt very stupid, not knowing what to do. Get undressed? Just like that? I thought: first I should kiss her. In the movies the man always kisses the woman before making love to her. I stepped toward her, looked at her intensely, then harshly pulled her toward me and kissed her on the mouth for a long time. Instinctively I had closed my eyes. When I opened them I saw hers, and in them an animal-like terror. This made me draw back a step.

"What's the matter?" I asked her, my heart beating.

"Nothing," she answered; her voice came from another world. "Nothing. Come. Let's make love."

All of a sudden she brought her hand to her mouth. Her face became white as if all life had left it.

"What's the matter with you? Say something!"

She didn't answer. Her hand on her mouth, she was looking through me as if I were transparent. Her eyes were dry, like a blind child's.

"Have I offended you?" I asked.

She didn't hear me.

"Do you want me to leave you?"

She was far away, taking refuge where no stranger was allowed. I could only be present outside. I understood that by kissing her I had set in motion an unknown mechanism.

"Say something," I begged her.

My plea didn't reach her. She looked mad, possessed. Maybe I had only lived for this meeting, I thought. For this meeting with a prostitute who preserved within her a trace of innocence, like madmen who in the midst of their madness hold on to a trace of lucidity.

This lasted a few minutes. Then she seemed to wake up; her hand fell from her face. A tired and infinitely sad smile lit up her features.

"You must forgive me," she said softly. "I spoiled everything. Excuse me. It was stupid of me."

She began to undress, but I no longer felt like making love to her. Now I only wanted to understand.

"Wait," I told her. "Let's talk a little."

"You no longer want to make love?" she asked worried.

"Later," I reassured her. "First let's talk a little."

"What would you like to talk about?"

"About you."

"What do you want to know?"

Mechanically she unhooked her skirt.

"Who are you?"

"A girl. A girl like many others."

"No," I protested. "You're not like the others."

She let her skirt fall to the floor. Now she was unbuttoning her blouse.

"How do you know?" she asked.

"Intuition probably," I answered awkwardly.

Now she was only wearing a black bra and pants. Slowly she stretched out on the bed. I sat down next to her.

"Who are you?" I asked again.

"I told you. A girl, a girl like many others."

Unconsciously I was stroking her hair.

"What is your name?"

"It doesn't matter."

"What is your name?"

"Sarah."

A familiar sadness took hold of me.

"Sarah," I said. "A beautiful name."

"I don't like it."

"Why not?"

"Sometimes it frightens me."

"I like it," I said. "It was my mother's name."

"Where is she?"

I was still stroking her hair. My heart felt heavy. Should I tell her? I couldn't pronounce such simple, such very simple words: "My mother is dead."

"My mother is dead," I said finally.

"Mine too."

Silence. I was thinking of my mother. If she saw me now . . . She would ask me:

Who is this girl?

My wife, I would say.

And what is her name?

Sarah, Mother.

Sarah?

Yes, Mother. Sarah.

Have you gone mad? Have you forgotten that I too am called Sarah?

No, Mother. I haven't forgotten.

Then, have you forgotten that a man has no right to marry a woman who bears his own mother's name? Have you forgotten that this brings bad luck? That a mother dies from this?

No, Mother. I haven't forgotten. But you can no longer die. You are already dead.

That's true. . . . I am dead. . . .

"Do you really want to know?"

Sarah's voice brought me back to earth. She was looking straight ahead, as if she were looking through walls, years, and memories, in order to reach the source, where the sky touches the earth, where life calls for love. Sarah put this question to me as if I, by myself, had created the universe.

"You really want to know who I am?"

Her voice had become hard, pitiless.

"Of course," I answered, hiding my fear.

"In that case . . ."

There are times when I curse myself. I shouldn't have listened. I should have fled. To listen to a story under such circumstances is to play a part in it, to take sides, to say yes or no, to move one way or the other. From then on there is a before and an after. And even to forget becomes a cowardly acceptance.

I should have run away. Or put my hands over my ears. Or thought about something else. I should have screamed, or sung, or kissed her, kissed her on the mouth so she would have stopped talking. Made love to her. Told her that I loved her. Anything, just so she would have stopped talking. So she would have stopped talking.

I did nothing. I listened. Attentively. I was sitting on the edge of the bed, next to her half-undressed body, listening to her story. My clenched fingers were like a vise around my throat.

Now, every time I think of her, I curse myself, as I curse those who do not think of her, who did not think of her at the time of her undoing. Her inscrutable face was like a sick child's. She looked straight ahead without fear, piercing the walls as if she could see the chaos that preceded the creation of the world.

I think of her and I curse myself, as I curse history which has made us what we are: a source of malediction. History which deserves death, destruction. Whoever listens to Sarah and doesn't change, whoever enters Sarah's world and doesn't invent new gods and new religions, deserves death and destruction. Sarah alone had the right to decide what is good and what is evil, the right to differentiate what is true from what usurps the appearance of truth.

And I was sitting next to her half-naked body, and listening. Each word tightened the vise. I was going to strangle myself.

I should have left. Fast. Fast. I should have fled when she opened her mouth, as soon as I noticed the first sign.

I stayed. Something was holding me back. I wanted to suffer with her. To suffer the way she was suffering. I also felt that she was going to humiliate herself. Maybe that prevented me from leaving. I wanted to take part in her humiliation. I was hoping her humiliation would fall back on me too.

She spoke and I listened in silence. Sometimes I felt like screaming like an animal.

91

Sarah spoke in an even, monotonous voice, stopping only to let silence comment upon an image that words would have been too weak to evoke. Her story opened a secret floodgate within me.

I knew there had been Sarahs in the concentration camps. I had never met any, but I had heard of them. I didn't know their faces were those of sick children. I had no idea that some day I would kiss one of them on the mouth.

Twelve years old. She was twelve years old when, separated from her parents, she had been sent to a special barracks for the camp officers' pleasure. Her life had been spared because there are German officers who like little girls her age. Who like to make love to little girls her age.

Suddenly she turned her darkened eyes toward me: God was still in them. The God of chaos and impotence. The God who tortures twelve-year-old children.

"Did you ever sleep with a twelve-year-old woman?" she asked me.

Her voice was calm, composed, naked. I tried not to scream. I couldn't justify myself. It would have been too easy.

"But you have felt like it, haven't you?" she asked when she noticed I kept quiet. "All men feel like it."

My eyes burned from her stare. I was afraid to scream. I couldn't justify myself. Not to her. Especially not to her. She deserved better.

"Tell me," she went on in a somewhat softer voice. "Is that why you're not making love to me? Because I'm no longer twelve?"

The God of impotence made her eyes flame. Mine too. I thought: I am going to die. Whoever sees God must die. It is written in the Bible. I had never quite understood that: why should God be allied with death? Why should He want to kill a man who succeeded in seeing Him? Now, everything became clear. God was ashamed. God likes to sleep with twelve-year-old girls. And He doesn't want us to know. Whoever sees it or guesses it must die so as not to divulge the secret. Death is only the guard who protects God, the doorkeeper of the immense brothel that we call the universe. I am going to die, I thought. And my fingers, clenched around my throat, kept pressing harder and harder, against my will.

Sarah decided to let me breathe a moment. She again looked straight ahead and went on talking as if I didn't exist or as if I alone existed, everywhere and always.

"He was drunk. A drunken pig. He was laughing. He stank of obscenity. Especially his laugh. 'It's my birthday today,' he said. 'I want a present. A special present!' He examined me from head to toe and snickered, 'You'll be my birthday present.' I didn't understand the meaning of his words. I was twelve. At that age you don't know yet that girls can be offered as birthday presents. . . . I wasn't alone in the barracks. A dozen women stood around us. Bertha was white. So were the others. White. Like corpses. He alone, the drunkard, was red. His hands too, like the butcher's. And his laughter went from his mouth to his eyes. 'You'll be my birthday present, you!' he said. Bertha was biting her lips. She was my friend."

She was a beautiful and sad-looking woman. She carried her head like an Oriental princess. The night she arrived in the camp, she had lost her daughter who was about Sarah's age.

"She's too young, sir," she interceded. "She's only a child."

"If she's here it means she is no longer a child," he had

93

answered, winking. "Otherwise, she would be you know where. Up there. . . ."

His fat finger pointed to the ceiling.

"Bertha was my friend," Sarah said. "She didn't give up. She fought to the end. To save me she was ready to take my place. The others too for that matter."

Sarah was silent for a moment.

In the half-darkness of the barracks, Bertha tried to divert him. Without saying a word, she began to undress. The other women—brunettes, blondes, redheads—without consulting one another did the same. In a flash they were all naked like silent, motionless statues. Sarah thought it was a bad dream, a sick nightmare. Or that she had gone mad. An inhuman silence had come over the barracks, contrasting vividly with the tenseness on the women's faces. Outside, the sun was moving behind the horizon spilling its rusty blood over the moving shadows. It seemed that if the scene went on something terrible would happen at any moment; something that would shatter the universe, change the course of time, unmask destiny, and allow man to see at last what awaits him beyond truth, beyond death.

That's when the drunkard caught the child by the arm and brutally pulled her outside the barracks. It was already dark. A reddish glow rose from the earth filling the sky with the deep color of blood.

"The officer was intelligent," Sarah said. "Among all the naked women who were in the barracks he had chosen me, although I was dressed. Because I was twelve. Men like to make love to women who are twelve."

Again she turned her head toward me and the vise tightened around my throat with renewed vigor.

"You too," she said. "If I were twelve, you would have made love to me."

94

I couldn't listen to her any more. I had reached the end of my strength, and I thought: one more word and I'll die. I'll die here, on this bed, where men come to sleep with a golden-haired girl and in fact don't know that they are making love to a twelve-year-old child.

For a brief moment I had the idea that perhaps I should take her right away. Abruptly. Without gestures, without useless words. To show her that one could fall still lower. That mud is everywhere and has no bottom. I got up slowly, took her hand, and kissed it gently. I wanted her to see. I wanted her to realize that I wanted her. That I desired her. That I too did not transcend the limits of my body. I placed my lips on her cold hand.

"That's all?" she asked me. "You don't want to do anything else?"

She laughed. She was trying to laugh like the other one, like the drunkard in the barracks. But she didn't succeed. She wasn't drunk. There was nothing obscene in her hands, or in her voice. She was as pure as one could be.

"I do," I answered shaken.

Bending over her, I kissed her on the mouth again. She didn't return my kiss. My lips were sealed on hers, my tongue was looking for hers. She remained passive, absent.

I straightened up and after a short hesitation I said very slowly, "I'll tell you what you are. . . ."

She tried to talk but I didn't give her a chance.

". . . You are a saint. A saint: that's what you are."

A flash of surprise crossed her sick and childlike face. Her eyes looked clearer. More cruel.

"You are mad!" she said violently. "You are really mad!"

And, letting loose, she laughed again. She imitated someone laughing. But her eyes didn't laugh. Nor did her mouth.

"Me, a saint!" she said. "You are out of your mind. Didn't I tell you how old I was when I had my first man? How old I was when I embarked on my career?"

She stressed the word "career," looking defiant as she asked her question.

"Yes," I said. "You did tell me. Twelve. You were twelve."

She was laughing more and more. It's the drunkard, I thought. He hasn't left her yet.

"And in your opinion," she went on, "a woman who starts her career at twelve is a saint? Right?"

"Right," I said. "A saint."

I thought: let her cry. Let her scream. Let her insult me. Anything would be better than this laugh which belongs to someone else, to a body without a soul, to a head without eyes. Anything would be better than this foreign and harmful laugh which turns her into a possessed soul.

"You're mad," Sarah said in a voice that tried to be gay and joyous. "The drunkard was only the first. After him came the others. All the others. I became the 'special present' of the barracks. The 'special present' that they all wanted to give themselves. I was more popular than all the other women combined. All the men loved me: the happy and the unhappy, the good and the bad, the old and the young, the gay and the taciturn. The timid and the depraved, the wolves and the pigs, the intellectuals and the butchers, all of them, do you hear? All came to me. And you think I am a saint. You are out of your mind, you poor man."

And she laughed even more. But the laugh had nothing to do with her. Her whole being brought to mind an ageless, nameless suffering. Her laugh sounded dry, inhuman: it wasn't hers, but God's or the drunkard's.

"You poor man!" she said. "I pity you! I would like to do something for you. Tell me, when is your birthday? I'll have a present for you. A special present. . . ."

And her laugh settled in me. Someday I too will be possessed. Sarah, in her black underwear, one leg slightly bent, suddenly stopped laughing. I felt the final blow was coming. Instinctively I started moving back toward the door. That's where I heard her scream.

"You're mad!"

"Be quiet! For heaven's sake, be quiet!" I shouted.

I knew she would talk, that she would tell me something terrible, abominable, words that I would always hear whenever I tried to find happiness in a woman's body.

"Be still!" I begged.

"A saint, me?" she screamed like a madwoman. "I want you to know this and remember it: sometimes I felt pleasure with them. . . . I hated myself afterwards and even while it lasted, but my body sometimes loved them. . . . And my body is me. . . . Me, a saint? Do you know what I really am? I was telling you. I am——"

I had reached the limit. I couldn't take it any more. I was going to throw up. Quickly I unlocked the door and opened it as fast as I could. I had to get out of that house at once. Second floor. First floor. Doorman. The street. Run. Fast. Run.

Only later, while running, did I notice that my fingers were still clutching my throat.

"Sarah," I said in a choked voice.

"Yes," Kathleen said. "It's your mother's name. I know."

"It's the name of a saint."

I spent days and weeks looking for Sarah. I went back to the café where I had met her. I asked in every hotel in the neighborhood. To no avail. Nobody seemed to have seen or known the golden-haired girl who bore my mother's name. The waiter who had served us did not remember. The hotel doormen all said they had never seen her. And yet I didn't give up hope. Sometimes I think I'm still looking for her. I would like to meet her, if only once. To do what I should have done that afternoon: make love to her.

"Your mother is dead," Kathleen said.

She wanted to hurt herself. Suffer openly. So I would see. So I would know that she was suffering with me, that we were bound together by suffering. She was able to hurt me just to show me that she too was unhappy.

"I know she is dead," I said. "But sometimes I refuse to admit it. Sometimes I think that mothers can't die."

It's true. I can't believe my mother is dead. Perhaps because I didn't see her dead. I saw her walking away with hundreds of people who were swallowed up by the night. If she had told me, "Good-bye, my son. I'm going to die," perhaps I could believe it more now.

Father is dead. I know that. I saw him pass away. I don't look for him among the people in the street. But sometimes I look for my mother. She's not dead. Not really. Here and there I see one of her features in some woman on the subway, on a bus, in a café. And these women, I love and hate them at the same time.

Kathleen. Tears were coming to her eyes. My mother didn't cry. At least not when other people were there. She only offered her tears to God.

Kathleen looked a little like my mother; she had her high forehead, and her chin had the same pure lines. But Kathleen wasn't dead. And she was crying.

In the beginning she didn't cry. We were on the same level. We dealt with each other like equals. We were free. Each one free from himself and free from the other. When I didn't feel like keeping a date, I didn't. She did the same. And neither of us was angry or even hurt. When I didn't talk for a whole night, she didn't try to make me explain. The familiar question asked by lovers, "What are you thinking about?" didn't enter our conversations. Hardness had become our religion. Nothing was said that wasn't essential. We tried to convince each other that we could live, hope, and despair, alone. Each kiss could have been the last. At any moment the temple could have collapsed. The future didn't exist since it was useless. At night we made love silently, almost like our own witnesses. A stranger watching us in the street could easily have taken us for enemies. Rightly so, perhaps. True enemies aren't always the ones who hate each other.

I shouldn't have said I'd see her again in New York. I should have told her that it wasn't worthy of us to reopen the parentheses: air moving into it would make everything rot.

She had changed. Kathleen was no longer free. She only imitated the other. Her marriage had destroyed her inside. She had lost all interest in life. The days were all alike. People all said the same thing. Instead of listening to them, you could follow TV programs. Her husband's friends and colleagues bored her. Their wives got on her nerves; she saw herself sentenced to become one of them. Very soon.

In New York, we met every day. She came to my place. I went to her place. We went out a lot, to the theatre, to concerts. We discussed literature, music, poetry. I tried to be nice. I was patient, kind, understanding. I treated her as if she were ill. The fight had been over for a long time. Now I was trying to help her get back on her feet.

We seldom evoked the past and only with caution, so as not to tarnish it. Sometimes as we listened to a passage from Bach, or noticed the shape of a cloud playing with the sun, we were seized by the same emotion. She would touch my hand and ask me, "Do you remember?"

And I would answer, "Yes, Kathleen. Of course. I remember."

Before, she would never have felt like proving to me that she remembered. On the contrary, we both would have felt ashamed to have fallen prey to the past, to an emotion from the past. I would have turned my head away. I would have talked about something else. Now we no longer struggled.

Then one day, she confessed. . . .

We were drinking coffee in her room. On the radio Isaac Stern was playing the Beethoven violin concerto. We had heard it in Paris at the Salle Pleyel. I remembered that she had taken my hand and that I had pushed her away brusquely. If she would take my hand now, I thought, I wouldn't pull it away.

"Look at me," Kathleen said.

I looked at her. She had a tormented smile. She had the face of a woman who has been abandoned and is conscious of it. She was tapping on the cup with her long fingers.

"Yes," I told her. "I remember."

She put down the cup, got up, and knelt before me. There, without lowering her head, without blushing, in a firm voice—almost as she used to be—she told me, "I think I love you."

She was going to continue but I interrupted her. "Be quiet!" I told her harshly.

I didn't want to hear her say: I have loved you since the first time we met.

My harshness was not reflected on her face. But her smile had become a little deeper, a little more sickly.

"It isn't my fault," she apologized. "I tried. I struggled."

Beethoven, the Salle Pleyel, Stern, love. Love that makes everything complicated. While hate simplifies everything. Hatred puts accents on things and beings, and on what separates them. Love erases accents. I thought: here's another minute that will punctuate my existence.

"Are you sad?" Kathleen asked, distressed.

"No."

Poor Kathleen! She was no longer trying to imitate her other self. Her face was covered with anguish. Her eyes had become strangely small.

"You're going to leave me?"

Love and despair. They go together. One contains some trace of the other. I thought: she must have suffered a lot.

101

It is my turn to try to repair the damage. I have to treat her as if she were ill. I know. To do this is to insult her other self. But the other self doesn't exist. No longer exists. And this one is broken.

"I'm not going to leave you," I answered in the voice of a faithful friend.

A tear slid down her cheek. "You pity me," Kathleen said.

"I don't pity you," I said eagerly.

I was lying. I would have to lie. A lot. She was ill. It is all right to lie to sick people. To her other self I would not have lied.

During the following weeks and months, Kathleen wasted away.

Having nothing to do—she neither felt like working nor needed to work—she spent her days in her room, at her window, or in front of a mirror, alone and unhappy, conscious of her solitude, of her unhappiness.

As before, we went on seeing each other every evening. Dinners, shows, concerts. Once I tried to reason with her: she was wrong to feel sorry for herself. It wasn't worthy of her or of me. She should find some work, be busy, fill up her days. She had to find an aim in life.

"An aim," she said, shrugging her shoulders. "An aim. What aim? The Salvation Army? Be a patron of starving artists? Go to India to help the lepers? An aim? Where would I look for it?"

That's when I had an idea. I told her that I loved her too.

She refused to believe it. She demanded proof. I proved it to her. All the incidents that in the past had shown that there was no love between us, now, all of a sudden, showed the contrary. "Why did you pull away your hand at the

102

concert?" "I didn't want to betray myself." "Why didn't you ever tell me that you loved me?" "Because I loved you." "Why did you always look me right in the eyes?" "To discover my love mirrored in them."

For weeks she was on her guard. And so was I. I considered myself her nurse. Sometimes I toyed with the thought that perhaps she too was treating me like a sick person. Someday we would take off our masks. One of us would say: I was only playing. So was I, the other would answer. And there would be a bitter taste in our mouths. But then it was a pity this was only a game.

However, she wasn't playing. If you play you do not suffer. The part of us which observes us, which watches us play, does not suffer. Kathleen had suffered. In spite of my arguments, she wasn't convinced. She often cried while I was away. When we were together her good spirits were too forced.

I was no longer free. My freedom would have humiliated Kathleen, who had been without freedom for so long. I had invented an attitude toward her which I could no longer get rid of.

If only this had done some good! If only it had helped Kathleen! But she was still unhappy and her laugh was still without sincerity.

Kathleen was getting worse and worse. She began to drink. She was letting herself go.

I discussed this with her. "You have no right to act this way."

"Why not?" she would say, her eyes wide open with an expression of false innocence.

"Because I love you. Your life matters to me, Kathleen."

"Come on! You don't love me. You just say so. If it were true you wouldn't say it."

103

"I'm saying it because it is true."

"You're saying it out of pity. You don't need me. I don't make you feel good or happy."

These arguments had none of the results I hoped for. On the contrary, after each one, Kathleen let herself go still further.

Then one evening—the day before the accident—she explained to me at last why she couldn't believe in the integrity of my love.

"You claim you love me but you keep suffering. You say you love me in the present but you're still living in the past. You tell me you love me but you refuse to forget. At night you have bad dreams. Sometimes you moan in your sleep. The truth is that I am nothing to you. I don't count. What counts is the past. Not ours: yours. I try to make you happy: an image strikes your memory and it is all over. You are no longer there. The image is stronger than I. You think I don't know? You think your silence is capable of hiding the hell you carry within you? Maybe you also think that it is easy to live beside someone who suffers and who won't accept any help?"

She wasn't crying. That night she hadn't been drinking. We were in bed. Her head was resting on my outstretched arm. A warm wind was blowing through the open windows. We had just gone to bed. This was one of our rituals: never to make love right away; to talk first.

I could feel how heavy my heart had become, as if it were unable to contain itself. She had guessed correctly. You cannot hide suffering and remorse for long. They come out. It was true: I was living in the past. Grandmother, with her black shawl on her head, wasn't giving me up.

"It isn't my fault," I answered.

I explained to her: a man who tells a woman he thinks

he loves, "I love you and shall love you forever; may I die if I stop loving you," believes it. And yet one day he sounds his heart and finds it empty. And he stays alive. With us—those who have known the time of death—it's different. There, we said we would never forget. It still holds true. We cannot forget. The images are there in front of our eyes. Even if our eyes were no longer there, the images would remain. I think if I were able to forget I would hate myself. Our stay there planted time bombs within us. From time to time one of them explodes. And then we are nothing but suffering, shame, and guilt. We feel ashamed and guilty to be alive, to eat as much bread as we want, to wear good, warm socks in the winter. One of these bombs, Kathleen, will undoubtedly bring about madness. It's inevitable. Anyone who has been there has brought back some of humanity's madness. One day or another, it will come to the surface.

Kathleen was sober and lucid that evening. I had the impression her old self had come to visit her. But I knew that it would leave again. That the visit would be short and that only the self that was trying to imitate it would remain. And someday even that one would stop searching. Then the divorce would be final.

That night I understood that sooner or later I would have to leave Kathleen. To stay with her had become meaningless.

I told myself: suffering pulls us farther away from other human beings. It builds a wall made of cries and contempt to separate us. Men cast aside the one who has known pure suffering, if they cannot make a god out of him; the one who tells them: I suffered not because I was God, nor because I was a saint trying to imitate Him, but only because I am a man, a man like you, with your weaknesses, your cowardice, your sins, your rebellions, and your ridiculous ambitions; such a man frightens men, because he makes them feel ashamed. They pull away from him as if he were guilty. As if he were usurping God's place to illuminate the great vacuum that we find at the end of all adventures.

Actually it is good that this should be so. A man who has suffered more than others, and differently, should live apart. Alone. Outside of any organized existence. He poisons the air. He makes it unfit for breathing. He takes away from joy its spontaneity and its justification. He kills hope and the will to live. He is the incarnation of time that negates present and future, only recognizing the harsh law of memory. He suffers and his contagious suffering calls forth echoes around him.

One day or another I shall have to leave Kathleen, I decided. It will be better for her. If I could forget, I would stay. I cannot. There are times when man has no right to suffer.

"I suggest an agreement," Kathleen said. "I'll let you help me, provided you let me help you. All right?"

Poor Kathleen! I thought. It's too late. To change, we would have to change the past. But the past is beyond our power. Its structure is solid, immutable. The past is Grandmother's shawl, as black as the cloud above the cemetery. Forget the cloud? The black cloud which is Grandmother, her son, my mother. What a stupid time we live in! Everything is upside down. The cemeteries are up above, hanging from the sky, instead of being dug in the moist earth. We are lying in bed, my naked body against your naked body, and we are thinking about black clouds, about floating cemeteries, about the snickering of death and fate which are one and the same. You speak of happiness, Kathleen, as if happiness were possible. It isn't even a

106

dream. It too is dead. It too is up above. Everything has taken refuge above. And what emptiness here below! Real life is there. Here, we have nothing. Nothing, Kathleen. Here, we have an arid desert. A desert without even a mirage. It's a station where the child left on the platform sees his parents carried off by the train. And there is only black smoke where they stood. They are the smoke. Happiness? Happiness for the child would be for the train to move backward. But you know how trains are, they always go forward. Only the smoke moves backward. Yes, ours is a horrible station! Men like me who are in it should stay there alone, Kathleen. Not let the suffering in us come in contact with other men. We must not give them the sour taste, the smoke-cloud taste, that we have in our mouth. We must not, Kathleen. You say "love." And you don't know that love too has taken the train which went straight to heaven. Now everything has been transferred there. Love, happiness, truth, purity, children with happy smiles, women with mysterious eyes, old people who walk slowly, and little orphans whose prayers are filled with anguish. That's the true exodus. The exodus from one world to the other. Ancient peoples had a limited imagination. Our dead take with them to the hereafter not only clothes and food, but also the future of their descendants. Nothing remains below. And you speak of love, Kathleen? And you speak of happiness? Others speak of justice, universal or not, of freedom, of brotherhood, of progress. They don't know that the planet is drained and that an enormous train has carried everything off to heaven.

"So, you accept?" Kathleen asked.

"I accept what?" I wondered.

"The agreement I suggested."

"Of course," I answered absent-mindedly. "I accept."

"And you'll let me make you happy?"

"I'll let you make me happy."

"And you promise to forget the past?"

"I promise to forget the past."

"And you'll think only about our love?"

"Yes."

She had gone through her questionnaire. She stopped to catch her breath and asked in a different tone of voice, "Where were you before?"

"At the station," I said.

"I don't understand."

"At the station," I said. "I was at the station. It was very small. The station of a small provincial town. The train had just left. I was left alone on the platform. My parents were in the train. They had forgotten me."

Kathleen didn't say anything.

"At first I was resentful. They shouldn't have left me behind, alone on the platform. But a little later, I suddenly saw a strange thing: the train was leaving the tracks and climbing toward the smoke-gray sky. Stunned, I couldn't even shout out to my parents: What are you doing? Come back! Perhaps if I had shouted, they would have come back."

I was beginning to feel tired. I was perspiring. It was warm in the bed. A car had just screeched to a stop under the window.

"You promised not to think about it any more," Kathleen said in despair.

"Forgive me. I won't think about it any more. In any case, these days trains are an outmoded way to travel. The world has progressed."

"Sure?"

"Sure."

She pressed her body against mine.
"Every time your thoughts take you to the little station, tell me. We'll fight it together?"
"Yes."
"I love you."
The accident occurred the next day.

The ten weeks I spent in a world of plaster had made me richer.

I learned that man lives differently, depending on whether he is in a horizontal or vertical position. The shadows on the walls, on the faces, are not the same.

Three people came to see me every day. Paul Russel came in the morning; Kathleen in the evening; Gyula in the afternoon. He alone had guessed. Gyula was my friend.

A painter, of Hungarian origin, Gyula was a living rock. A giant in every sense of the word. Tall, robust, gray and rebellious hair, mocking and burning eyes; he pushed aside everything around him: altars, ideas, mountains. Everything trembled, vibrated, at his touch, at the sight of him.

In spite of our difference in age, we had a lot in common. Every week we would meet for lunch in a Hungarian restaurant on the East Side. We encouraged each other to stick it out, not to make compromises, not to come to terms with life, not to accept easy victories. Our conversation always sounded like banter. We detested sentimentality. We avoided people who took themselves seriously and particularly those who asked others to do so. We didn't spare each other. Thus our friendship was healthy, simple, and mature.

I was still half dead when he burst into my room, pushed the nurse aside with his shoulder (she was getting ready to give me an injection), and, without asking me anything, announced in a firm and decided voice that he was going to do my portrait.

The nurse, needle in hand, stared at him aghast.

"What are you doing here? Who let you in? Get out immediately!"

Gyula looked at her with compassion, as if her mind were not all there.

"You're beautiful," he told her. "But mad!"

He studied her with interest.

"Beautiful women nowadays aren't mad enough," he went on nostalgically. "But you are. I like you."

The poor nurse—a young student—was on the verge of tears. She was stuttering.

"The injection— Get out— I have to——"

"Later!" Gyula ordered.

And taking her by the arm, he pushed her toward the door. There, she whispered something in his ear.

"Hey! You!" Gyula said after closing the door. "She says you are seriously ill. That you're dying! Aren't you ashamed to be dying?"

"Yes," I answered weakly. "I'm ashamed."

Gyula walked about to familiarize himself with the view, the walls, the smell of the room. Then he stopped near the bed and challenged me.

"Don't die before I've finished your portrait, do you

hear? Afterwards, I don't give a darn! But not before! Understood?"

"You're a monster, Gyula," I told him, moved.

"You didn't know?" he wondered. "Artists are the worst monsters: they live on the lives and deaths of others."

I thought he would ask how the accident had happened. He didn't. And yet, I wanted him to know.

"Do you want me to tell you about it?" I asked him.

"You don't have to," he answered disdainfully. "I don't need your explanations."

There was a circle of fondness around his eyes.

"I want you to know," I said.

"I'll know."

"It's a secret," I said. "No one knows it. I'd like to tell you."

"You don't have to," he answered contemptuously. "I like to discover everything for myself."

I tried to laugh. "I might die before you have a chance."

He was flaming with threatening anger. "Not before I'm through with your portrait, I told you. Afterwards you can die whenever and as often as you like!"

I was proud. Proud of him, of myself, of our friendship. Of the tough laws we had made for it. They protected us against the successes and the certainties of the weak. True exchanges take place where simple words are called for, where we set out to state the problem of the immortality of the soul in shockingly banal sentences.

Gyula turned up every afternoon. The nurses knew they weren't to disturb us when he was there. For them he was an animal whose insults, in Hungarian, would have reddened even the cheeks of a black girl.

While he was sketching, Gyula told me stories. He was an excellent storyteller. His life was filled with innumerable adventures and hallucinatory experiences. He had died of hunger in Paris, handed out fortunes in Hollywood, taught magic and alchemy nearly everywhere. He had known all the great men of contemporary literature and the arts; he liked their weaknesses and forgave them their successes. Gyula too had an obsession: to pit himself against fate, to force it to give human meaning to its cruelty. But of course he only spoke of that mockingly.

One day he came as usual toward the beginning of the afternoon, and, framed by the window, began to work. He was silent. He hadn't even said hello when he came in. He seemed preoccupied. Half an hour, an hour. He suddenly stopped moving, remained motionless, and looked me straight in the eyes, as if he had just torn asunder an invisible veil that covered them. For a few seconds we stared at each other. His thick eyebrows arched as he frowned: he was beginning to understand.

"Do you want me to tell you?" I was upset.

"No," he answered coldly. "I have no use for your stories!"

And again he was absorbed by his work in which he found answers to all questions and questions for all answers.

A week later he told me something that didn't seem to have any relation to the subject we were then discussing. We were speaking of the international situation, the danger of a third world war, the important part that China would soon be playing. Suddenly Gyula changed the subject.

"Incidentally," he said, "have I told you the story of my unsuccessful drowning?"

"No," I answered mockingly. "Where did it happen: in China?"

"Spare me your comments," he said. "You'd do better to listen."

Good old Gyula! I thought. How do you tell a woman that you love her? You probably insult her, and if she doesn't understand that kind of love-talk, you simply stop loving her. Good old Gyula!

One summer he had gone to the French Riviera for his vacation, to get away from the heat. He often went to the seashore. That morning he swam out too far. Suddenly a sharp cramp paralyzed his body. Unable to use either his arms or his legs, he let himself sink.

"I began to drink the salt water of the sea," he said. "There was no fear in me. I knew that I was dying, but I remained calm. A strangely sweet serenity came over me. I thought: at last I'll know what a drowning man thinks about. That was my last thought. I lost consciousness."

He was saved. Someone had seen him sink and rescued him.

While watching the lines his brush drew on the canvas, Gyula went on, smiling imperceptibly.

"When I came to, I looked all around me. I was lying on the sand, in the midst of a group of curious people. A bald old man, a doctor, was leaning over me and taking my pulse. In the first row, a terrified young woman was looking at me. She put on a vague smile for me, but the expression of terror remained. How distressing: a horrified woman who smiles. I thought: I'm alive. I have outwitted death. One more time death didn't get me. Here is the proof: I'm looking at a woman who is looking at me and smiling. The horror on her face is there for death which must still be very near, right behind me. The smile is for me, for me alone. I told myself: I could have been here, in the same spot, and not have seen this woman, who, right now, is more graceful and beautiful than any other. I could have been looked at by a woman who didn't smile. I must consider myself happy, I told myself. I'm alive. Victory over death should give birth to happiness. Happiness to be free. Free to provoke death again. Free to accept freedom or to reject it. This reprieve should give me a feeling of well-being. And yet, I didn't have it. I was searching conscientiously within myself: not a trace of joy to be found. The doctor was examining me, the people gave me mute expressions of sympathy like alms, and the young woman's smile was becoming more open—that's how one smiles at life. In spite of that, I wasn't happy. On the contrary, I was terribly sad and disappointed. Later, this unsuccessful drowning made me sing and dance. But there, on the sand, under the burning, purple sun, under the eyes of this unknown woman, I felt disappointed, disappointed at having come back."

Gyula worked silently for a long time. I think he was painting with his eyes closed. I was wondering if he was still disappointed. And if later on he had seen the young woman again. But I said nothing. Paul Russel came back to my mind. He is wrong, I thought. Life doesn't necessarily want to live. Life is really fascinated only by death. It vibrates only when it comes in contact with death.

"Will you listen to me? Gyula, will you?" I implored.

He jumped up as if I had just forced him to reopen his eyes. There was a little sardonic laugh.

"No, I won't," he said.

"But I'd like you to know."

"To know what?" he asked harshly.

"Everything."

"I don't need your stories in order to know."

Good old Gyula! I thought. What happened to the young

woman on the beach? Did you insult her? Did you tell her, "You are a little bitch, a dirty little bitch?" Did she understand that these were words of love?

"Gyula," I asked him, "what happened to the unknown woman?"

"What unknown woman?"

"The one on the beach. The one who smiled at you?"

He was overcome by a loud laugh that must have been hiding a wave of tenderness surging up in him from the distant past.

"Oh, that one?" he said in a voice that tried to sound vulgar. "She was a little bitch, a dirty little bitch!"

I couldn't help smiling. "Did you tell her that?"

"Of course I told her!" He realized I was smiling. "You monster," he shouted at me in disgust. "Let me work. Otherwise I'll beat you up!"

The day before I was supposed to leave the hospital, Gyula came in surrounded by an aura of arrogance. He stood like a victorious general at the foot of my bed, between the river and me, and announced the good news: the portrait was finished.

"And now, you can die," he said.

Gyula placed it on a chair. He hesitated for a second. Then, turning his back to me, he stepped aside. My heart was beating violently. I was there, facing me. My whole past was there, facing me. It was a painting in which black, interspersed with a few red spots, dominated. The sky was a thick black. The sun, a dark gray. My eyes were a beating red, like Soutine's. They belonged to a man who had seen God commit the most unforgivable crime: to kill without a reason.

"You see," Gyula said. "You don't know how to speak; you are yourself only when you are silent."

He quivered slightly, unable to hide his emotion.

"Don't talk," he added. "That's all I'm asking you."

And to hide, he went to the window and looked at the playful waves of the East River moving elegantly toward their date with infinity.

He had guessed. It was enough to look at the painting to realize. The accident had been an accident only in the most limited sense of the word. The cab, I had seen it coming. It had only been a flash, but I had seen it, I could have avoided it.

A silent dialogue now took place between Gyula and me.

"You see? Maybe God is dead, but man is alive. The proof: he is capable of friendship."

"But what about the others? The others, Gyula? Those who died? What about them? Besides me, they have no friends."

"You must forget them. You must chase them from your memory. With a whip if necessary."

"Chase them, Gyula? With a whip, you said? To chase my father with a whip? And Grandmother? Grandmother too, chase her with a whip?"

"Yes, yes, and yes. The dead have no place down here. They must leave us in peace. If they refuse, use a whip."

"And this painting, Gyula? They are there. In the eyes of the portrait. Why did you put them there if you ask me to chase them away?"

"I put them there to assign them a place. So you would know where to hit."

"I can't, Gyula. I can't."

Gyula turned and all of a sudden I saw that he had grown older. His hair had become white, his face thinner, more hollow.

"Suffering is given to the living, not to the dead," he

117

said looking right through me. "It is man's duty to make it cease, not to increase it. One hour of suffering less is already a victory over fate."

Yes, he had grown older. It was now an old man talking to me and handing over to me the ageless knowledge that explains why the earth is still revolving and why man is still looking forward to tomorrow. Without catching his breath, he went on as if he had saved these words for me for a long time.

"If your suffering splashes others, those around you, those for whom you represent a reason to live, then you must kill it, choke it. If the dead are its source, kill them again, as often as you must to cut out their tongues."

A boundless sadness came over me. I had the impression I was losing my friend: he was judging me.

"What if it cannot be done?" I asked him, feeling very dejected. "What should one do? Lie? I prefer lucidity."

He shook his head slowly.

"Lucidity is fate's victory, not man's. It is an act of freedom that carries within itself the negation of freedom. Man must keep moving, searching, weighing, holding out his hand, offering himself, inventing himself."

All of a sudden I had the impression that it was my teacher, Kalman the cabalist, who was talking to me. His voice had the same kind, understanding accent. But Kalman was my teacher, not my friend.

"You should know this," Gyula went on without changing his tone of voice, without even blinking an eye, "you should know that the dead, because they are no longer free, are no longer able to suffer. Only the living can. Kathleen is alive. I am alive. You must think of us. Not of them."

He stopped to fill his pipe, or perhaps he had nothing

118

else to add. Everything had been said. The pros and the cons. I would choose the living or the dead. Day or night. Him or Kalman.

I looked at the portrait and hidden in its eyes I saw Grandmother with her black shawl. On her emaciated face she wore an expression of peaceful suffering. She was telling me: *Fear nothing. I'll be wherever you are. Never again shall I leave you alone on a station platform. Or alone on a street corner of a foreign town. I'll take you with me. In the train that goes to heaven. And you won't see the earth any more. I'll hide it from you. With my black shawl.*

"You're leaving the hospital tomorrow?" Gyula asked in a voice that sounded normal again.

"Yes, tomorrow."

"Kathleen will take care of you?"

"Yes."

"She loves you."

"I know."

Silence.

"You'll be able to walk?"

"With crutches." I answered. "They took off the cast. But I can't put any weight on my leg. I have to walk with crutches."

"You can lean on Kathleen. She'll be happy if you lean on her. Receiving is a superior form of generosity. Make her happy. A little happiness justifies the effort of a whole life."

Kathleen will be happy, I decided. I'll learn to lie well and she'll be happy. It's absurd: lies can give birth to true happiness. Happiness will, as long as it lasts, seem real. The living like lies, the way they like to acquire friendships. The dead don't like them. Grandmother would not accept

119

being told less than the truth. Next time, I promise you Grandmother, I'll be careful. I won't miss the train again.

I must have been staring at the portrait too intensely because all of a sudden Gyula started gritting his teeth. With an angry, enraged motion, he took a match and put it against the canvas.

"No!" I exclaimed in despair. "Don't do that! Gyula, don't do it! Don't burn Grandmother a second time! Stop, Gyula, stop!"

Gyula, unmoved, didn't react. His face closed and withdrawn, he was holding the canvas with his finger tips, turning it in all directions, and waiting for it to be reduced to ashes. I wanted to throw myself on him, but I was too weak to get out of the bed. I couldn't hold back my tears. I cried a long time after Gyula had closed the door behind him.

He had forgotten to take along the ashes.